Wisdom of Nana via Gebo Passage

"Three grand essentials to happiness in this life are something to do, something to love, and something to hope for."

Joseph Addison (English Writer 5-1-1672-6-17-1719

By Ben Rayman

Contents

"A bird doesn't sing because it has an answer, it sings because it has a song."

Maya Angelou

Art-to-Art Palette Books

Published by Art-to-Art PaletteBooks, an imprint of:
Media House Communications
Ohio City, Ohio 45874-9230
Web: arttoartpalette.com

Publisher's Notice:
This is a work of fiction. Names, characters, places, images and incidents are either a product of the author's imagination or are used factiously. Any resemblance to actual persons, living for dead, business establishments, events or locales is entirely coincidental.

First Novel Printing
2025 Copyright © recorded
Book Design by Art-to-Art Palette Journal staff
Manufactured in the United States of America
Designated official published date May 23, 2025

Wisdom of Nana via Gebo Passage

Reviewers have called this novel a narrative with *"strong emotional resonance and a clear narrative arc."* They praise how *it "effectively introduces the core characters and their situation, setting the stage for future developments,"* and how the themes of *"change, connection, home, and the impact of global events on personal lives are well-established."*

∞∞

A Tapestry of Cultures and Humanity: Follow the intertwined stories of the Grabowsky, Cohan, Cohen, and Smith families, each carrying rich cultural heritages that shape their destinies. From the innocence of young love to the turbulence of political upheaval, their journeys reveal how generosity, fairness, and mutual support can forge hope even in the darkest times.

∞∞

An Emotional and Spiritual Odyssey: This novel gently guides you through triumphs and trials, exploring themes of family, faith, cultural identity, and resilience. You'll feel the heartbeat of their stories, as they navigate life's challenges amidst global conflicts and personal dreams—making their victories all the more inspiring.

"*Dawn Fog*"

To Dad

*"The best portion of a good man's life is his little, nameless,
unremembered acts of kindness and of love."*

William Wordsworth 1770-1850

*"One thing that stirs me when
I look back at my youthful
days is the fact that so many
people gave me something or
were something to me without
knowing it.
Such people with whom I
have, perhaps, never exchanged
a word, yes, and others about
whom I have merely heard
things by report, have had a
decisive influence upon me; they
entered into my life and became
powers within me…
Hence I always think that we
all live, spiritually, by what
others have given us in the
significant hours of our life."*

Albert Schweitzer

To Murray

*"I don't like work, no man does, but I like what is in work;
the chance to find yourself, not for others, but what no
other man can ever know."*

Joseph Conrad 1857-1924

Foreword

Wisdom of Nana via the Gebo Passage was originally written and published in 2019 as a short story read. It was presented to only touch upon certain life parts within the whole: Family, Faith, Cultural Heritage and Career as well as to provide the reader with a glimpse of an eventual novel.

The reader would also find what I imagine with some detail in other parts such as in chapter, *"Back Home for Vacation"* was only the tip of what they themselves can add to its visual portrait.

During my initial years in the publishing industry, my tasks were not solely limited to one specific role because there weren't any stops after the story has been covered and written.

Before it reaches the readers and such as phrased in the industry: *"Put to bed"* — there are such main production segments: Composing, Camera, Press and Circulation. Of course, in the beginning I did not follow these paths individually, but it was relatively a short time before *"Getting my feet wet"* was no longer a 'duh' — I knew what to do next and if there was a delay; there were always other parts that kept me moving.

Mainly from 1970 and before I took the *'I Do'* leap in May 1975, my days and nights were like one because of the sheer volume of growth, led by a young publisher who was fulfilling his own business aspirations, which I describe as a decade business plan; achieved in a standard five-year projection.

Today when I step back in time, I know what was

not asked, was easy for me to give because I was raised to take the lead and tote the 'cross of responsibility' for the others who could or would not.

Of course, I had another personality quirk and that environment fed my unrelenting need to know how. Furthermore, I was in search of my own community voice and I had it in the bag several times, but my genetic entrepreneurialism led to other related, including non-related off-shoot paths in publishing.

However as Ralph Waldo Emerson once said, *"Do not go where the path may lead, go instead where there is no path and leave a trail."* The lanes to me may not be lined in greenbacks, but I do know the *Art-to-Art Palette Journal* is a publication rich in content and gigantic in paying forward. It will achieve its rightful place in history and right along those recorded for their special gifts.

For those who found the original short story release of the *Wisdom of Nana via Gebo Passage*, including the other *Portraits of Life* short stories that was included, I thank you for taking that initial journey with me.

As Cher once put it, *"If grass can grow through cement, love can find you at every time in your life."* Today, you are invited to travel along with Benjamin and the many people who have entered his world as well as their personal struggles, successes, family histories, relationships and the person-to-person dialogs they voice in pursuit about what they are doing and is worth living for in this expansion of **Wisdom of Nana via Gebo Passage** to its full-length novel. ♥

Ben Rayman

"Windy Point"

The Road Not Taken

Two roads diverged in a yellow wood,
And sorry I could not travel both
And be one traveler, long I stood
And looked down one as far as I could
To where it bent in the undergrowth;

Then took the other, as just as fair,
And having perhaps the better claim,
Because it was grassy and wanted wear;
Though as for that the passing there
Had worn them really about the same,

And both that morning equally lay
In leaves no step had trodden black.
Oh, I kept the first for another day!
Yet knowing how way leads on to way,
I doubted if I should ever come back.

I shall be telling this with a sigh
Somewhere ages and ages hence:
Two roads diverged in a wood, and I—
I took the one less traveled by,
And that has made all the difference."

Robert Frost

"A Beacon to Freedom"

PRELUDE OF THE PASSAGE

"Take the first step in faith. You don't have to see the whole staircase, just take the first step."

Martin Luther King Jr.

L ong before I set eyes on Jackie Coleman, the Gift Rune revealed that a partnership in some form was at hand. My grandmother, Marganita 'Maggie' Cohen-Grabowsky, was deeply involved in predicting the future, and throughout my childhood and youth, I was her main subject.

I can recall those sessions vividly, but one night stands out sharper than the rest.

I was seven years old.

The fall season had begun, and the evening air carried the distinct crispness of autumn. The house was settling into its nightly quiet, the occasional creak of wood the only sign of life beyond the glow of the fireplace in the sitting room.

Then, I heard Nana's voice.

"Benjamin, come to me."

There was no urgency in her call—only certainty as if she had been expecting this moment long before I was even born.

I hesitated for a brief second before climbing out of bed. The hall was dim, but I knew the way. I had walked it countless times, always feeling a strange sense of separation the moment I reached her door, as if stepping into a place outside of time.

I knocked once.

Her voice thundered from the other side.

"Enter."

Then, just as quickly, it softened into her usual low, melodic murmur *"my son."*

I pushed open the heavy door.

A thick wave of sweet herbal potpourri hit me immediately, strong enough to sting my eyes. The air was thick with it, mingling with the ever-present scent of burning wax and something older—earthy, bitter, familiar.

The candles scattered across the room burned low, their golden flames flickering wildly, casting long, shifting shadows against the wooden walls. It made the edges of the room blur, giving the impression of a sky full of distant stars.

I blinked, my vision momentarily dazed by the effect.

Nana stood before the fireplace.

She was dressed differently than usual—not in her familiar layered skirts and beaded shawls, but in a full-length white robe, pristine against the fire's glow. She had

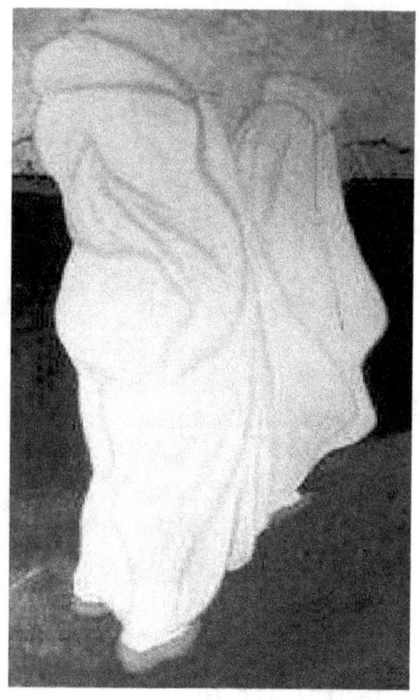

her arms crossed, and something in her stance struck me as authoritative, unmoving.

I wasn't used to seeing her this way.

I cocked my head slightly.

"Gee! You look like God," I muttered.

A slow, knowing smile spread across her face, glowing in the firelight.

"Come," she said, motioning toward the small wooden stool beside her table.

I stepped forward, still rubbing the slight sting from my eyes, and felt her hand gently guide me toward our secluded world.

The crystal ball sat at the center of her table, a smooth, polished orb, its depths unreadable. I had seen her use it many times, her fingers gliding over its surface, her lips moving in hushed tones as if listening to whispers beyond my hearing.

Tonight, however, there was no slow, deliberate preparation.

Tonight, she already knew what she was looking for.

She placed both hands over the crystal, her fingers barely touching its surface. The fire crackled behind her, and for a long moment, there was only silence.

I shifted slightly, waiting for the usual performance—the murmured phrases, the mysterious half-smiles, the riddles she always wove into her predictions.

At first, it was just that.

She began her usual litany of my future, reciting the same vague fortunes she had always given me.

"A good life, a fine wife, many children..."

I let my mind drift.

I had heard it all before. The same practiced phrases, the same promises of happiness, the same reassurances that my path would be smooth, fruitful, and full of purpose.

But then—she stopped.

Mid-sentence.

The shift was immediate, as sudden as if someone had cut the string of a tautly pulled bow.

I looked up, expecting her to continue.

But Nana's eyes had changed.

Her focus was no longer on me, nor even on the crystal. Her pupils had widened, and her breathing had slowed. The skin around her mouth tightened.

She wasn't speaking anymore.

She was seeing.

A cold sensation crawled up my spine, an instinctive response to something I couldn't quite name.

I sat perfectly still.

The room felt too quiet. Though still burning, the fire no longer crackled the way it had moments ago. It was as if the air itself had thickened, held in place by something unseen.

Then—her voice returned.

Only this time, it was different.

Lower. Slower. Unshakable.

"You will travel east, far to the east. You will learn a

new life and find your calling there. And there you will meet your true love."

Unbeknownst to me, I can't imagine myself pondering who would be my chosen or even what it meant to have a true human love, mainly because of my early school-age and my true love was always leaving enough time for play, die-cast model cars, and the *Barrel of Monkeys* toy.

I am sure I probably echoed something like, "Wow Wee Nana. You can see all that in that ball? Do you see Santa bringing me a *Mighty Tractor*?"

"No, Benjamin. The Gift Rune does not reveal future toys for you," said Nana.

As the smoke thickened, Nana peered more deeply into the ball.

"There is much going on. I see many other people in your aura, even a tractor slowly moving in a field in the far distance. It is plowing the ground."

Nana spoke in her deep voice, "Looks very much like your Grandad Asa Grabowsky when he was your age. We lived next door. Asa always helped my dad, Peter Cohen in the garden. They worked tiredly side-by-side, no complaining."

The garden was huge, and Grandad Cohen was

always planting a variety of new vegetables and flowers and sharing the garden's bounty, especially with Grandad Asa's family.

"So you see me as a farmer in the future on my Mighty Tractor? Hotdog!" said Benjamin.

I always liked going to the Saginaw County Elevator with Grandad Asa. Time has aged it because of its worn, dilapidated look with the musty, smoky smells flowing in its airways.

From the outside, the elevator also had a spooky feeling, which I recall when going into those haunted houses alone during the Leelanau County Fair.

Oddly, I was never in fear; I was just intrigued by what the ghouls would do to get me to scream, yet they did keep me on edge, uptight, not knowing when they were going to pounce, and when they did, it released a repetition of happy laughs.

A second later, she was back to her old self, Nana,

the fortune-teller, rattling on about how I would do well in school.

"My favorite subject is making pictures with mosaics. I might also become an artist like Mom," quipped Benjamin.

"The Runes has spoken to me at this time. We will revisit as you blossom in age," sternly said Nana.

I did not yet understand it.

But I would.

One day, I would.

Camouflages in Motion

As I advanced in age in the 1980s, the world bustled forward, forging ahead with its unceasing march of progress, though much of it seemed to pass by me as nothing more than noise on the wind.

The clamor of political machinations in Washington and abroad was distant, a world away from the one I inhabited. Neither the election of Ronald Reagan, who became our 40th US President, nor the world's first elected female president, Vigdís Finnbogadóttir for Iceland stirred any deeper sentiment in me than passing interest. Even the tragic and senseless assassination of John Lennon, the man whose voice had once echoed an era's restless yearning, struck me only in fleeting sadness before fading into the chorus of history's steady hum.

The great technological revolutions, the burgeoning personal computer era that promised to alter life as it had always been known, barely raised a ripple in my day-to-day existence. But with its hypnotic, ceaseless chase, Pac-Man offered more intrigue than the broader implications of digital progress. I recall those endless hours spent with childhood friend Billy Atenwood.

"Come on. Benny. eat'em up," Billy would bellow as Pac-Man raced through the maze.

"I am! The ghosts are on my tail," said Ben in a shouting tone.

However, I would not come to appreciate this mindless pleasure, it wasn't until some years later, around the time that the silver screen bore witness to the gentle melancholy of E.T. the Extra-Terrestrial, a tale that would serve as an eerie foreshadowing of my own life's path—of reunions long-awaited, of the partings that never quite severed the thread that bound two souls across time and distance.

Through all the noise of a world forever shifting, one thing remained steadfast: the sacred tradition of the family. Our Thanksgiving feasts were not merely meals but tributes to the many bloodlines and histories that had converged upon this singular point in time.

Every dish, painstakingly prepared from scratch, was more than sustenance — it was an heirloom, a whisper from ancestors whose hands had once kneaded the same dough, stirred the same broths, and seasoned the same meats with the same old-world reverence. It was a banquet that would have suited even the most opulent of Lucullan feasts, a gathering of indulgences born not of excess but of unwavering devotion to tradition.

The very air was thick with the mingling scents of braised meats, yeasted bread, and simmering stews, an intoxicating medley of French, Dutch, Jewish, German, and Irish origins. The sweet tang of spiced cider, the savory perfume of slow-roasted game, the buttery decadence of delicate pastries — each flavor bore the distinct fingerprint of the past, a lineage woven through generations.

But the food was merely the backdrop, the canvas upon which our greatest tradition played out — the recounting of our history, the retelling of long -buried stories that had lived only in sepia-toned photographs, and the hushed whispers of elders.

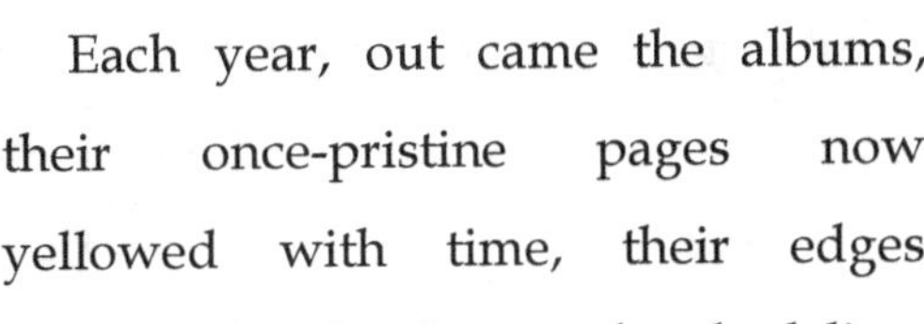

Each year, out came the albums, their once-pristine pages now yellowed with time, their edges softened by the fingers that had lingered upon them year after year. Unbeknownst to us, these sessions were not mere reminiscing but acts of

preservation, a battle against time's slow and relentless erosion. The past was not content to remain buried — it demanded to be spoken, brought forth through laughter, sighs of remembrance, and the quiet reverence of those who listened with unspoken understanding.

What surfaces now are a few memories, I could speak of without end. My mother's sister, Esther, possessed Hedy Lamarr's striking beauty, though it was softened by a homespun warmth akin to Dolly Parton's affable charm. There was a brightness to her, a warmth that made her presence feel less like a person and more like a comforting hearth on a bitter winter's night.

Although my dad was an only living biological child, Nana and Asa became foster parents for Ginny. Her parents, Thomas and Sara Morgret-Brinkman sought the same as others, and were in their late 30s when they emigrated from France. Sara befriended Nana during her early days in Traverse City. They became family, a sister each never had and both Dad and Ginny became not only cousins, but also little brother and big sister when tragedy struck.

A semi lost its brakes coming down a steep incline, pushing Ginny's parent's pickup off the road, tumbling to the bottom, exploding into flames. Once Asa and Nana heard of the accident and the details, they rushed to the Brinkman home to comfort Ginny from the onslaught of sorrow.

She lived with us for the next four years and Nana and she would work tirelessly to connect Ginny with her French relatives which they found in Paris. Dad always recalled when the mailman would bring packages and letters from France because of all the stamps and markings.

After high school graduation, Ginny who could speak French fluently, Nana, Asa and Dad saw her off to France to re-connect with her biological family.

Ginny had the luminous allure of Lana Turner, but her spirit was cut from the same cloth as Ann Richards, that unyielding Texan force of nature who could command a room with nothing but the steel in her voice and the twinkle in her eye.

Their husbands, too, were cut from distinct but complementary cloths. Esther's Oscar, ever the benevolent soul, had a quiet dignity about him, the kindness of a Jimmy Carter, who saw people as they were and accepted them without judgment or expectation. Ginny's Tom, ever the optimist, bore a likeness to Bill Clinton in his unwavering belief in possibility, in his warm-hearted nature, in his way of lifting those around him without ever demanding recognition for the act.

But beyond the faces frozen in old photographs, beyond the laughter and stories that wove themselves into the fabric of these gatherings, there were two figures whose presence loomed largest in my world, my father and Murray.

They were not merely men of influence in my life; they were the architects of my understanding of the world, the steady hands that had molded me, knowingly or not, into the man I was becoming. Like my life partner today, they embodied an unshakable truth—that though the path forward may be uncertain, it is not ours to see clearly. We walk by faith, not by sight.

And so, as I drift back to my youth, as I recall that Thanksgiving of the 1980s, I remember how the passage of time seemed to collapse upon itself. Each day spent among family did not feel like a continuation, but rather a melding of past and present, a convergence of lifetimes so intertwined that one could not distinguish where one began and the other ended.

It was then that I understood — truly understood —
Nana's wisdom.

She had always seen further than the rest of us. She
had rolled the Runes, peered into her crystal orb, and
glimpsed not only the shape of my fortunes but the truths
that would define my existence. She had spoken of my
successes and my path enterprise world. But beyond the
material, she had seen something far more immutable. This
unbroken thread that connected me to another.

A partnership, she had called it. One forged in
youth, tempered by time and bound by fate long before we
had the words to name it.

As I stood before Jackie, eyes meeting hers again
after decades apart, I felt that truth settle deep into my
bones.

There had never been a goodbye, only a pause.

There had never been distance, only waiting.

The proverb is wrong. Absence does not make the
heart grow fonder — it merely confirms what the heart has
always known.

Jackie had been there all along — waiting.

And so had I.

"A Light in the Forest"

GRANDPARENTS UNION

"I can honestly say that I was never affected by the question of the success of an undertaking. If I felt it was the right thing to do, I was for it regardless of the possible outcome."

Golda Meir

♥

Nana and Grandpapa Asa Grabowsky had been bound together since childhood, their love woven into the very fabric of their survival. They were teenage sweethearts, but their courtship was anything but simple. There were no leisurely strolls into an easy life, no quiet afternoons dreaming about the future without the shadow of war looming over them. Their story was shaped by unrest, by the kind of choices that defined not just who they were but who they would become.

Russia was no longer safe. By 1935, the world around them was shifting rapidly. Stalin's regime had already begun tightening its grip, and though Hitler had not yet invaded, the whispers of war had already reached St. Petersburg. People spoke in hushed tones about what was coming—the political purges, the mass arrests, the growing tension between nations. Choices had to be made. To stay was to risk everything. To leave was to gamble on the unknown.

Grandpapa's voice always lowered when he told the story, as if, even decades later, the weight of that moment still pressed against his chest.

"It was late autumn," he would begin, his weathered hands resting on his knees, eyes distant. "The wind off the river carried a bite, and the streets were alive with movement. Merchants were unloading goods, dock workers bent under the weight of heavy sacks  of grain, and stray dogs sniffed between the wooden planks of the docks for scraps."

Ships lined the harbor—foreign vessels among them, their flags snapping in the cold wind. Some bore the red and white of Poland, others the Union Jack, but one ship stood apart from the rest. Its hull was made of dark steel, towering over the others, and painted boldly along its side was a name neither of them would forget.

Freedom's Destiny.

A fitting name, though they wouldn't understand its significance until much later.

"As we walked," Grandpapa continued, "I saw an officer nailing a sign to the dock's post, his breath curling in the cold air." He paused, shaking his head with a half-smile—the kind of expression that only comes with looking back on a moment that changed everything.

"The sign said they were looking for a cook and a ship chandler to journey to China and back."

Asa had no experience as a cook, but he could learn. Nana had grown up in a family that valued survival skills above all else. She could barter, she could manage supplies, and most of all, she could adapt.

She frowned at the sign, pulling her wool shawl tighter around her shoulders. "China," she murmured, testing the word on her tongue. "That is far from here."

"Far is what we need," Asa replied. His fingers brushed over hers, a silent promise between them.

Nana hesitated, glancing back at the city that

had been their home for so long. "What if we never return?"

Asa exhaled, his breath a ghost in the cold air. "Then, at least we'll have a chance at something else."

Neither of them knew then that this decision would change the course of their lives.

They didn't know that six months at sea would turn into years. They didn't know that war would spread its shadow across Europe while they were thousands of miles away. They didn't know that they would meet people who would become family, or that their love story would not just survive but thrive aboard a ship.

But in that moment, standing on the edge of a decision they could not take back, Asa reached for Nana's hand, and she held on tight.

"Though I was only seventeen, I knew this was it. Our way out."

Grandpapa Asa's voice carried the weight of that realization—the certainty that when fate opens a door, hesitation can mean the difference between escape and entrapment. He had spent his whole life in a city that no longer belonged to him, watching as fear crept into the lives of those around him. There was no time to be a boy anymore. This was the moment to become a man.

He squared his shoulders and approached the officer. His heart pounded, but he didn't let it show. He wasn't just asking for a job—he was seizing a future.

"I told Captain Tirone Smith I was nineteen—and he believed me," Grandpapa said, his smile widening. "I was already tall, broad-shouldered. The kind of boy who had worked with his hands since childhood. I looked older, carried myself older—and that was all that mattered."

Captain Smith stood on the dock, a striking figure against the backdrop of *Freedom's Destiny*, a golden sunset that painted the sky in hues of orange and pink. The wind tousled his dark hair, which, despite his youth, was speckled with hints of salt from the sea. He wasn't much older than Asa—not yet touched by the deep lines that marked the faces of seasoned sailors, but clearly molded by the sea's demands. His jaw was strong, and his eyes, a piercing shade of blue, held the depth of a thousand uncharted waters. Each glance spoke of a practical wisdom beyond his years, tempered by the relentless rhythm of life on the ocean.

"Ever worked on a ship before?" His voice echoed with authority, a no-nonsense tone that belied the boyish twinkle in his eye, a gaze that danced with the thrill of adventure.

"Yes, sir," Asa lied smoothly.

The captain's mouth twitched with a slight upturn at the corners of his mouth, suggested he was perpetually on the edge of laughter, as if he saw through the lie but chose not to question it. As he studied Asa, his sharp gaze seemed to assess more than just experience; it evaluated potential, igniting a spark in the young man that hinted at endless possibilities.

"You may just have the makings of a fine seafarer," he said, his tone shifting slightly, revealing warmth beneath the stern exterior. "Let's find out together. We leave in the morning."

But there was one problem.

He wasn't leaving without Nana.

"She was everything," Asa said simply. "There was no future if it wasn't with her."

Nana, in her usual way, didn't flinch. She never hesitated. She knew, just as he did that this was the moment they had been waiting for, whether they had known it or not.

When they returned home, she pulled him aside, her dark eyes fierce with determination. "We do this together, Asa. No matter what."

He nodded. "Always."

But there was still the issue of getting her on board. They needed a story — something that would make sense, something no one would question.

"Papa introduced me as his new bride," Nana would say later, a flicker of amusement dancing in her eyes. "We told them we were building a nest egg for our future, that we wanted to see the world before we settled down."

It was a lie — but a necessary one.

The truth was far more desperate.

There was no time to second-guess.

They ran home, breathless from the cold and from the enormity of what they were about to do. There was no discussion, no drawn-out goodbyes.

"We packed quickly — a few clothes, a handful of photographs, especially those of her grandparents, and my father's pocket watch. That was all," Nana said. She hesitated, fingers running over the small locket around her neck. Inside was a picture of her mother and father. "I told myself I'd come back for them one day."

Nana's mother, Rebecca Rose Greenbaum was born in Vienna Austria in 1899, she had an elegance, a refinement, a look of royalty. These qualities were reflected in the spotless home she kept; treasures of glassware, pottery, paintings were artfully displayed as well as those personal jewelry and clothing mementos she wore.

"My grandmother would tell me her family roots were connected to Henry VI when he ruled during the 12th century," said Nana.

Her father, Peter Solomon Cohen had no knowledge of his family before him, only his parents. He had a no-nonsense stern personality, yet hidden behind those facial expressions was a husband who treated his wife like a Queen, who he called Beckie Rose. When it came to his children, he shielded them from the rise of political aggressions because of their Jewish heritage, wanting them to only relish in its goodness.

"Grandpa Pete farmed the land like his parents," Nana said. The Cohen's were hard workers, from sun-up to nightfall. "Their farm always gave me a feeling of a circus. So many animals from cows, sheep, pigs, chickens, goats," added Nana.

But that was not all, annually they sowed nearly 100 acres of corn, wheat and soybeans. Nana continue to reminisce about her Grandmother's garden. "She taught me her secret ways how to plant, when and what vegetables were ready to pick which graced the table during family meals."

The hardest part wasn't leaving Russia.

It was leaving family behind.

But even then, their parents understood.

"Your great-grandparents didn't put up a fuss," Nana admitted, her voice quieter when she spoke of that moment. "They knew. They had seen the warnings long before we did. They could already feel the weight of something terrible coming."

Her mother held her tight at the door, whispering in her ear, "Go, my love. Go before it's too late."

Her father gripped Asa's his shoulder. "Be strong. Protect her."

And then it was done.

Asa did not have any memories of his grandparents because his parents fled from Lithuania before he was born during World War I. Yet, his goodbyes to his parents, was not as easy.

His father, Asher Grabowsky couldn't fight off the onslaught of emotions of his only son leaving, nor his older sisters of Charlotte, Abigail and Sarah. But his mother, Rachel Fischer-Grabowsky knew she had to embrace his leaving as a proud parent with a strong-ness as she did when she sent her only son off to school for the first time without her 'apron string' attached.

"I remember all six of us were in a huddle, heads bowed, arms around each other in a circle of solidarity, gazing down at a patch of peonies, flowers that symbolizes love, honor, good luck and prosperity," Asa said in a trembling voice tone.

The sisters were all rambling at once about the antics they would play on Asa. "I tied a string to his finger one night, ran it to my bed to pull so when Asa started to rock the bed, I would pull it to get him to stop," said Charlotte.

"I remember! You should remember me screaming loud and then the thunder of Dad's feet on the stair steps," said Asa.

Everyone had a memories which brought on the laughter as well as the tears, and when it was time for Asa to leave, each gave him their until we meet again hug, but his dad held onto him that seem like an eternity.

Asa's dad whispered into his ear, "You are my hero son. I will pray for you and Maggie for a better life and your return home."

By morning, Nana and Grandpapa were aboard *Freedom's Destiny*, watching the familiar shores of St. Petersburg shrink in the distance as the wind carried them toward a world they had never known.

They were young and foolish.

They were running toward the unknown.

And they had no idea they would never return.

The journey was meant to be temporary.

But history had other plans.

The sea was kind to them in the beginning.

Freedom's Destiny cut through the waters like a knife, smooth and steady, the wind filling its sails as though it, too, was eager to leave Russia behind. The deck swayed gently beneath their feet, the sun glittered off the rolling waves, and the air smelled fresh—crisp salt and damp wood mingling with the distant scent of fish.

For Nana, it was all new.

She stood at the rail, gripping the polished wood, her dark hair whipping across her face as she watched the sun sink below the horizon. St. Petersburg was gone now, swallowed by distance, replaced by an endless stretch of blue.

"Not bad, eh?" Asa leaned beside her, arms crossed over his chest, his eyes following the last sliver of light.

"It's beautiful," she admitted, voice barely above a whisper.

They were sailing westward, threading their way through the Baltic Sea, passing the Danish coast where Copenhagen's spires pierced the skyline. The ship stopped briefly there; the crew allowed a few hours of shore leave while merchants hauled crates of cured meats and barrels of rye aboard. The city was alive — market stalls bursting with fresh bread, children running barefoot along cobbled streets, the air rich with the scent of roasted chestnuts and warm pastries.

Asa managed to barter for two small apple tarts, warm and sticky with caramelized sugar.

"For you," he said, handing one to Nana as they leaned against a stack of wooden crates on the dock.

She took a bite, the flaky crust crumbling between her fingers. "You should have gotten more," she said through a mouthful, cheeks puffed.

He laughed. "I only had enough to trade for two. I figured you'd steal mine anyway."

She did.

From Copenhagen, they sailed along the North Sea, stopping at Rotterdam to take on crates of Dutch cheese and pickled herring. At every port, the cargo hold grew fuller, the ship lower in the water, its belly packed with goods destined for faraway shores.

The first few weeks felt like an adventure.

The crew — mostly a rough mix of Dutch, British, and Scandinavian sailors — welcomed Asa easily. He was strong, capable, and willing to work.

"You ever been at sea before, kid?" a burly Norwegian named Henrik asked one afternoon as they secured barrels of salted cod below deck.

Asa wiped the sweat from his brow. "No. But I've worked with my hands all my life."

Henrik grinned, clapping a heavy hand on his shoulder. "Good. The sea likes men who work. Lazy ones don't last."

Nana found her place in the galley, dodging the sharp orders of Ellis, the ship's cook, who barked at her to chop faster, stir harder, carry heavier. But beneath his gruffness, there was something almost protective about him.

"Don't let 'em push you around," he muttered once, shoving a bowl of soup into her hands. "Men get stupid on long voyages. Keep your wits."

She did.

The sea was kind to them—until they hit the Atlantic.

As the ship turned westward, leaving Europe behind, the days began to stretch.

Without ports to stop at, without fresh faces to greet them, without land in sight, the ship became a world of its own.

The air turned cold. The wind carried a bite, stinging their skin and making their clothes damp with salt. The waves swelled higher, the once-gentle rocking of the ship becoming an unpredictable, rolling lurch.

Nana clung to the rail some nights, her stomach twisting as the ship tilted sharply with each passing swell.

"How do you do this every day?" she groaned to Ellis, who was calmly chopping onions in the galley.

"You get used to it." He didn't look up.

"I don't want to get used to it."

He chuckled. "Then you'll have a miserable time, girl."

Even Asa, who had taken to ship life with an easy confidence, grew restless. When the day's work was done, there was nothing to do but wait. No streets to walk, no sights to see, no conversations beyond the same dozen faces that sat together night after night in the cramped mess hall.

It felt like a prison with walls of water.

Even the crew grew impatient, tempers flaring over meaningless things—who took the last piece of bread, who left a rope uncoiled, who spoke too loudly while others were trying to sleep.

"You ever been at sea this long?" Asa asked Henrik one evening as they sat on overturned barrels near the stern.

"Longer," the older man grunted. He pulled a knife from his boot and began whittling a small block of wood. "The worst is yet to come."

Asa frowned. "What do you mean?"

Henrik didn't look up. "Give it another two weeks. That's when the men start seeing ghosts."

Asa had taken to pacing the deck at night, hands in his pockets, the cold wind cutting through his shirt. Nana would sometimes join him, pulling her shawl tight around her shoulders, standing close enough for their arms to brush.

It wasn't all bad. They had each other. And they had found a rhythm in ship life—hard work, small comforts, quiet moments stolen in the dark.

But there were no secrets on a ship.

And Captain Smith wasn't a fool.

Late one evening, as the crew finished their supper and the mess hall buzzed with conversation, Ellis, the ship's cook, approached them with a nod.

"Captain wants a word with you two."

Nana froze, her spoon hovering over her bowl. Asa set his cup down carefully.

Ellis shrugged. "Nothing bad, I think. Just go."

They exchanged a glance before standing.

The captain's quarters were small but well-kept, the walls lined with maps and ledgers, a brass compass resting on the cluttered desk. A single lantern swung from the ceiling, casting flickering light over the worn wooden floor. The scent of cigar smoke clung to the air.

Captain Smith sat behind his desk, rolling a cigar between his fingers, watching them as they stepped inside. He didn't speak right away; just let the silence stretch.

Then, without looking up, he flipped through a logbook and muttered, "Alright. When did you two get married?"

Asa answered immediately.

"Five months ago."

"At the docks before we left."

Their words crashed into each other, two different answers spoken at the same time.

Silence.

"A Brand New Day"

A MARRIAGE AND A NEW LIFE

"It is a truth universally acknowledged, that a single man in possession of a good fortune, must be in want of a wife."

Jane Austen, From Pride and Prejudice, Chapter I

♥

The two lovers had bungled and knew that there was a price to pay. The captain had found out about their lie and now, who knew what was to come next?

Smith finally looked up, exhaling a long, slow breath through his nose. He didn't look angry. He looked… tired.

He set the cigar down and folded his hands in front of him. "So," he said dryly, "which one is it?"

Asa glanced at Nana. There was no point in lying.

He straightened his shoulders. "We're not married. Not yet."

Smith leaned back in his chair, rubbing his temple. "Well, that explains the awkward answers." He shook his head. "But what I don't get is—why? You're clearly in love. So why lie?"

Nana opened her mouth, then closed it.

Asa spoke first. "We didn't have a choice." He kept his voice steady, meeting the captain's gaze. "The ship was our only way out. If they knew Nana was alone, they wouldn't have taken her. This was our only chance to leave Russia together."

Smith studied him for a long moment. Then, to their surprise, he just sighed.

"There's nothing to worry about," he muttered, rubbing a hand over his face. "Nothing at all."

Asa blinked. "…Sir?"

Smith waved a hand. "Look, I've been at sea long enough to know that every man here has a story. Half of them aren't true. And the ones that are? Well, they're usually worse." He picked up his cigar again, rolling it between his fingers. "What I care about is my crew working hard and keeping their heads down. You two? You work hard. You don't cause problems. That's enough for me."

Nana let out a quiet breath. Asa nodded.

The captain gestured toward the door. "You can go."

They turned to leave, relief washing over them. But just as Asa reached for the handle, Smith spoke again.

"Wait."

They stopped.

The captain tapped his cigar against an ashtray, watching them with an unreadable expression.

"You two ever thought about making it official?"

Asa glanced at Nana, who looked up at him with wide, uncertain eyes.

"I have," Asa admitted.

Smith nodded slowly, as if he had expected that answer. "Good." Then he leaned forward, resting his elbows on the desk. "Because I can marry you."

Silence.

Nana's lips parted slightly. Asa's fingers twitched at his sides.

Smith smirked at their stunned expressions. "What? You thought all I did was steer the ship?"

They didn't know what to say.

Smith chuckled, shaking his head. "Think about it. Let me know."

And with that, the conversation was over.

As they stepped out into the corridor, the heavy

wooden door shutting behind them, Nana exhaled sharply.

"That was..." she trailed off.

"Unexpected," Asa finished for her.

She glanced up at him, searching his face. "What do you think?"

He didn't answer right away. He took her hand and squeezed it gently.

Then, softly, he said, "I think we should."

And Nana, after a beat, squeezed back.

The following days passed in a blur of work and quiet anticipation.

Word had spread among the crew that Captain Smith would perform a wedding ceremony on deck. It wasn't a grand event, nor an inconvenience—just another moment in the rhythm of ship life.

No one expected a grand celebration. There were no flowers, no silk dresses, but there was music—of sorts. A few of the crew had scraped together what they could; old Jakob, the ship's carpenter, pulled out a battered concertina, squeezing out a melody that was more enthusiasm than precision. One of the younger deckhands tapped out a rhythm on an overturned barrel, and someone else whistled along, off-key but cheerful. It wasn't much, just a rough, uneven tune carried by the wind, but for a moment, it felt like the ship itself was joining in the occasion.

It was enough.

On the evening of the ceremony, the sky stretched out endlessly above them, a deep navy canvas dotted with stars. The ship rocked gently beneath their feet as the crew stood in a loose circle, hands stuffed into pockets, boots scuffing against the worn wooden planks.

Asa wore his usual shirt even though all clean and tidied up for the event, the fabric slightly damp from the spray of the sea. Nana stood beside him in one of her best and tidiest dresses, her dark hair tied back loosely, the locket around her neck which bore her parents' pictures, and her father's watch wrapped around her hand. There was no need for finery — not out here, not with these people.

Captain Smith stood before them, his posture rigid, but something in his face — something almost imperceptible — had softened. A lantern swayed from the mast behind him, casting flickering shadows over his weathered face.

He cleared his throat, glancing at the gathered crew. "Alright," he muttered. "Let's get this over with."

A few chuckles rippled through the men, but then all fell silent.

Captain Smith cleared his throat, his gruff voice

cutting through the quiet hum of the sea.

"Marriage isn't about grand ceremonies or fine clothes. It's not about rings or riches. It's about waking up every day and choosing each other even when times are hard. Especially when times are hard."

Nana swallowed, her fingers tightening around Asa's.

Smith exhaled, glancing between them. "Alright, let's make this official." He turned to Asa first. "Asa Grabowsky, do you take this woman to be your wife? To stand by her, through fair seas and storms alike? To hold fast when the world turns against you and to walk beside her wherever this life takes you?"

Asa's grip on Nana's hands tightened. His voice was steady, unwavering. "I do."

Smith nodded, then turned to Nana. "Nana, do you take this man as your husband? To share in his burdens and his joys? To walk with him wherever the tides carry you, in dark waters and in calm?"

Nana drew in a slow breath, her heart pounding in her chest. But she already knew the answer. She had known it long before this moment.

"I do."

A quiet murmur passed through the crew, a few of

them shifting as if unprepared for the weight of those words.

Smith gave a firm nod. "Then say what you need to say."

Asa looked at Nana—not just at her face, but into her, as if seeing all the moments that had brought them here.

"I don't have fancy words," he admitted, voice low but firm. "I don't have promises wrapped in poetry. But I have this—I will stand by you. I will fight for you. I will be with you in whatever comes next." He exhaled, squeezing her hands. "I have nothing else in this world except you, Nana. And that's enough."

A lump formed in her throat, but she refused to cry.

Smith gave a small nod, then turned to Nana. "Your turn, girl."

She inhaled deeply, her voice quiet but unwavering.

"We left everything behind," she said, searching Asa's eyes. "Home. Family. The life we thought we'd have. And I thought, maybe, that would leave me feeling lost." She shook her head slightly. "But I don't feel lost. Because wherever you are, Asa—that's where I belong."

Silence settled over the deck, heavy but not uncomfortable. Someone in the crowd coughed, clearing his throat. A few of the men shifted, eyes darting away, as if the they weren't prepared to witness the depth of those words.

Captain Smith let the moment linger before clearing his throat. "Alright, then." He straightened his posture, his voice carrying over the gathered men.

"By the authority given to me as captain of this ship, I now pronounce you man and wife."

A beat of stillness.

Then, a loud cheer erupted from the crew. Someone clapped Asa hard on the back, nearly sending him stumbling forward. A flask was passed through the crowd, rough hands shoving it into Asa's grip.

"To the groom!" someone called.

"To the bride!" another voice echoed.

Laughter rolled through the salty air as Asa took a swig from the flask, the burn of cheap whiskey hitting his throat. He passed it to Nana, who hesitated before taking a small sip, grimacing at the taste. More laughter followed.

The celebration was brief—there was work to be done at dawn—but in those few moments, the ship wasn't just a vessel. It was a home.

The crew began to drift back to their quarters, leaving Nana and Asa standing together beneath the swaying lantern light.

She turned to him, her breath visible in the cool air. "So... we're married now."

Asa exhaled, a small smile tugging at the corner of his mouth. "Yeah. Looks like it."

She tilted her head, studying him. "Do you feel any different?"

He shook his head. "No. But I feel..." He hesitated, searching for the right word.

"...Settled," she finished for him.

He nodded slowly. "Yeah."

She stepped closer, resting her head against his shoulder.

They stood like that for a long time, listening to the waves, feeling the ship sway beneath them, knowing that they would face it together no matter what lay ahead.

They belonged to the sea now.

And to each other.

Honeymoon on Hold

In the hours after the wedding, they settled into a routine. The ship pressed forward across the vast Atlantic, stopping only where the sea allowed. Their marriage hadn't changed much in their daily lives—there was still work to do, still meals to cook, decks to scrub, sails to mend—but there was an unspoken certainty between them now. Whatever came next, they would face it together.

After months at sea, *Freedom's Destiny* reached her first major stop—China.

Shanghai in 1936 was a city caught between worlds. Western influence mingled with ancient traditions, and skyline was dotted with both grand colonial buildings and old Chinese temples. The harbor was a chaotic maze of junk ships, British steamers, and merchant vessels from every corner of the world.

Nana had never seen anything like it.

As they approached, she stood on the deck watching the teeming docks unfold before her. The air smelled of fish, coal smoke, and spices she couldn't name. Foreign words filled the air, shouted between dockworkers, traders, and sailors.

Asa leaned on the rail beside her. "You ever think we'd see a place like this?"

She shook her head. "Never."

Shanghai was a port of trade, and *Freedom's Destiny* was there to do business. The cargo was unloaded—barrels of salt fish, crates of textiles, and bundles of steel tools— while the ship took on new goods bound for Europe: teas, silks, and dried herbs. The crew was given two days of shore leave while supplies were restocked.

Nana and Asa spent most of it exploring the market streets, filled with rows of stalls selling dumplings, roasted meats, lacquered teapots, and fine embroidered fabrics. Knowing they were standing on the other side of the world from where they had begun was a strange feeling.

But there was no time to linger. The world was shifting, and the sea did not wait.

By the third morning, *Freedom's Destiny* pushed off from the Shanghai docks, carrying her new cargo and setting course for Europe.

The voyage westward was long, but by now, the rhythm of ship life had settled deep into Nana's bones. She knew the creak of the ship as she moved, the sounds of the waves hitting the hull, and the way the wind felt different depending on how close they were to land.

The journey home took even more months, stopping in India, through the Suez Canal, and across the Mediterranean, picking up more cargo before pushing north toward Holland.

By the time they reached Amsterdam, *Freedom's Destiny* needed more than just supplies. She needed repairs.

The engines had been struggling for weeks. Captain

Smith had done his best to keep them running, but the ship couldn't keep pushing westward without maintenance. Holland was their best option—a place where the ship could be docked, repaired, and readied for her final journey home.

Amsterdam was calmer than Shanghai—gray stone buildings lining narrow canals, bicycles rattling down cobbled streets, merchants selling tulips from wooden carts. But beneath that calm, the news from Europe was growing worse.

There were whispers of war, of Germany growing stronger, and of people disappearing. The letters they had once received from home had stopped coming.

One evening, as Nana served supper in the officer's mess, she overheard something that made her stomach drop.

Captain Smith sat at the head of the table, scanning the new set of orders he had received from the port authorities.

"We're not heading back to Russia," he said, voice flat. "New orders came in."

Asa, who had just entered with a tray of bread, froze.

Smith didn't look up. "We're picking up a shipment of cattle in Chicago. We're heading to America."

The words barely registered at first.

America.

That wasn't part of the plan.

Asa and Nana sat in silence in their cramped quarters later that night, the ship rocking gently against the Amsterdam docks.

"We were supposed to go home," Nana whispered.

Asa shook his head. "There's no home to go back to."

And he was right. Russia was no longer theirs. Even if they returned, what would be waiting for them? A country crumbling under the weight of war? A city they no longer recognized?

Nana exhaled slowly. "America, then."

Asa reached for her hand. "America."

There was no excitement in his voice, no dreams of riches or opportunity. It was just acceptance. The sea had carried them far from where they had started, and now it was pushing them toward a place they had never imagined going.

By the end of the week, *Freedom's Destiny* left

Amsterdam, her hull stocked with goods, her course set westward.

As the ship pushed into the open ocean, leaving Europe behind, Nana stood at the rail one last time, watching the distant shoreline disappear.

She didn't cry.

Because this time, she knew-she and Asa weren't just running anymore.

They were starting over.

What began as a desperate escape from the looming terrors of Hitler's rise turned into something far longer—a journey that stretched across continents and generations, shaping the course of their lives in ways neither Nana nor Asa could have foreseen. But they weren't the first to be carried across the ocean by forces beyond their control.

Chain of Acquaintances in Bloom

Captain Tirone Smith's family had made their own journey long before Asa and Nana ever set foot on *Freedom's Destiny*.

It was the winter of 1910 when Elizabeth Moreau stepped aboard a passenger ship bound for America, leaving behind the only home she had ever known.

She was barely 18, her heart torn between the weight

of farewell and the uncertain promise of what lay ahead. France had been left battered and broken in the aftermath of World War I. The economy had crumbled, entire villages had been lost to the fighting, and families like hers—once stable, once secure—found themselves with little left to hold on to.

Her parents, Pierre and Mary Louise Durand-Moreau, were unable to rebuild in the aftermath of the war, had made the painful decision to send her away, placing her in the care of relatives in Frankfort, Michigan— cousins, Jacques and Catherine Bonnet-Dubois, who had left France years before in search of work and stability.

"This is your chance," her mother had whispered at the dock, pressing a rosary into Elizabeth's hand. "A better life."

The ship was enormous, filled with immigrants from every corner of Europe—men and women carrying their entire lives in a single suitcase, clutching children's hands, whispering to one another in a dozen different languages. The voyage was cold, the North Sea choppy, the air thick with the smell of salt and unwashed clothes.

And that was where she met Edward Smith.

He had boarded in Southampton, England, and just was another young traveler bound for the unknown. He had spent his entire childhood in the dockyards of Liverpool, his father a shipbuilder, his mother a seamstress. The war had changed everything. Jobs had dried up, and with them, any future he had once imagined for himself.

So he left.

America, everyone had said, was the place for a fresh start.

Elizabeth had first noticed him while standing near the ship's rail, watching the gray expanse of the Atlantic stretch endlessly before them. He wasn't like the other young men aboard—he didn't push to make conversation, didn't boast about his plans for America. He simply stood beside her, his hands tucked into his coat pockets, eyes lost in the distance.

"Do you think it's true?" she asked suddenly, breaking the silence.

He turned his head slightly. "What?"

"That America is everything they say it is?"

Edward exhaled, the breath curling into the cold air. "I think it's different for everyone."

She studied him. "And for you?"

He shrugged. "Not sure yet."

It wasn't much of a conversation, but it was enough.

In the weeks that followed, their paths continued to

cross—on the deck, in the crowded dining hall, in stolen moments when neither of them could sleep and found themselves wandering the dim corridors of the ship.

Elizabeth had always been careful, always guarded. But there was something about Edward's quiet steadiness that made her feel safe in a way she hadn't expected.

By the time they reached Ellis Island, their names were called, and their documents were checked, they didn't part ways.

Elizabeth Moreau and Edward Smith had stepped onto American soil together, bound not only with the few belongings they carried and the shared weight of their pasts, but also by deep love for each other that blossomed. The many weeks at sea felt like months. They had left their homelands with nothing more than hope in search of a better life in America, yet they knew were meant to become one, and that was enough.

Their marriage was simple, a quiet ceremony held in the modest home of Elizabeth's relatives in Frankfort, Michigan. The war had taken much, but it had also given them something—a chance to build a new life, a life where their future was no longer dictated by forces beyond their control.

But fate, as always, had other plans. Their first and only child, Tirone Smith, was never meant to survive.

Elizabeth's pregnancy had been difficult from the beginning. The local doctor warned her of the risks, gently suggested that she rest, be careful, and perhaps not be strong enough to carry to term.

She didn't listen.

She had crossed an ocean. She had started over in a country that was not her own. She had built a life from nothing.

She wasn't going to let go now.

The night Tirone was born, the house was filled with the scent of candle wax and sweat, the air thick with the metallic tang of too much blood. The midwife, an older woman with steady hands and tired eyes, had worked tirelessly, but Edward could see it in her face—something was wrong.

Elizabeth's grip on his hand had been weak, her skin pale, her body trembling with exhaustion.

In the final moments of that long, harrowing night, she had looked at him then and whispered, "Promise me he'll be strong."

And then Tirone cried, his voice sharp and new, breaking through the suffocating silence.

The midwife had barely managed to stabilize

Elizabeth, had barely kept her from slipping away, but she had survived.

And so had their son.

Edward never spoke of that night. But Elizabeth—Elizabeth never forgot.

She raised Tirone with the fierce determination of a woman who had fought for his life and for her own.

From the time he could walk, Tirone was drawn to the water.

Frankfort is located on the shores of Lake Michigan and has a history of catering to commercial shipping. His father's work as a dock laborer kept them on shore often, Edward had left England behind, but he had never truly left the sea. It was in his blood, in his hands, in the way he tied knots absentmindedly when he sat at the kitchen table.

Tirone watched, learned, and imitated.

As a child, he would sit on the docks for hours, watching the merchant ships roll in, their towering masts cutting through the sky, listening to the rough voices of the men who worked them.

By the time he was 15, he had his first job on a cargo ship, scrubbing decks and hauling crates.

By 18, he was already a seasoned deckhand.

By 20, he had seen more of the world than most men twice his age.

He worked the Great Lakes first, then the Mississippi River, following the jobs, following the tides. But it was the ocean that called to him, that whispered of something more.

Tirone earned his captain's title the hard way—through grit, through work and through years of proving himself in a world where men had to fight for every opportunity.

He didn't come from money. He didn't come from power. He built himself from nothing, much like his parents before him.

By the time he took command of *Freedom's Destiny*, he was a man who had seen it all—storms that nearly swallowed ships whole, ports filled with broken men searching for purpose, sailors who had nowhere left to go.

And yet, for all he had seen, he never could have imagined the role he would play in someone else's escape.

Years later, when he unknowingly offered two young Russians a way out, he had no idea he was shaping history once again—just as his own parents had done before him.

<u>Journey Continues...</u>

As Nana and Asa's own voyage stretched, shaped by the unpredictability of history and the pull of destiny, they had no way of knowing how much of their path had been laid long before they ever set foot on *Freedom's Destiny*.

The sea had carried Elizabeth and Edward toward a new life.

And now, it had done the same for them.

When they first set foot in America, they were still just in their late teens. They believed they had only bought themselves time, a temporary refuge until the world calmed, and until they could return to Russia and pick up the pieces of the life they had left behind.

But history had no intention of giving them that chance.

The ship that had saved them from one fate had simply carried them toward another.

For the next three and a half years, *Freedom's Destiny* never remained still. The war in Europe raged on, growing worse with each passing month, and while the Atlantic became a battlefield of its own, Captain Smith took to safer waters, steering the ship inland, into the veins of America's great rivers.

The Mississippi. The Missouri. The Ohio.

The ship became something else—a workhorse, taking on low-wage contracts, hauling goods up and down the waterways, moving coal, grain, timber, and livestock from port to port.

Life on the rivers offered no sense of home.

No promises about where they would end up next.

"We saw the whole country from the water," Grandpapa would later say, his voice tinged with something between wonder and exhaustion. "From New Orleans to St. Louis, Memphis to Minneapolis. Places I never imagined I'd see. And all the while, we worked. Every day. Never resting, never staying."

The mighty rivers of America carried them deeper inland than they had ever imagined going.

In New Orleans, the docks smelled of salt and fish, mingling with the heavy perfume of magnolia trees and the lingering haze of tobacco smoke from the French Quarter. The ship's crew took leave for a single night, wandering the city's crowded streets filled with jazz music and voices in a dozen different languages. Asa and Nana sat on the docks, watching paddle steamers churn past, and their lights flickering against the water.

In St. Louis, they docked beneath the shadow of the

unfinished Gateway Arch, where men in heavy boots loaded barrels of flour and crates of canned goods onto the ship.

In Memphis, they walked along Beale Street, the sound of blues music drifting through the warm night air. The Mississippi moved sluggish and brown beneath the city's bridges, the riverboats humming in the distance.

Everywhere they went, the ship took what work it could.

The pay was low. The work was hard. And the future remained uncertain.

But they survived.

By the time *Freedom's Destiny* reached Chicago, nearly four years had passed.

They arrived under a heavy gray sky, the air thick with the smell of coal smoke and the distant scent of meatpacking plants. The docks bustled with workers. Their breath was visible in the chilly morning air, loading and unloading shipments bound for the Great Lakes.

This was meant to be just another stop. Another city. Another job.

But for the first time in years, Nana and Asa felt something they hadn't felt in a long time.

The need to stay.

They were no longer teenagers running from a war—they were adults who had spent nearly four years chasing survival. And for the first time, since they had stepped onto *Freedom's Destiny,* they felt the pull of something different.

The pull of solid ground.

The pull of a place to call home.

And Chicago, with all its grime and noise, crowded streets and endless promise, would be where they finally stepped off the ship—for good.

Nana knew before she even said it out loud—they were done with the sea.

She had felt the shift weeks before, the quiet certainty settling deep in her bones. It wasn't just the exhaustion of ship life, the endless rocking beneath her feet, or the cold, damp air that clung to her skin. It was the child.

Their child.

One evening, the realization struck her fully as she stood at the galley counter, rolling dough under her palms, the scent of flour and sea salt thick in the air. Her hands stilled, resting lightly on her stomach. A quiet smile tugged at her lips.

For years, she and Asa had moved wherever the tides carried them. The ship had been their home, its cramped quarters and wooden decks more familiar than solid ground. But a child needed more than waves beneath their feet. A child needed something steady, something certain. She had made up her mind before dinner was even served.

That night, the galley was filled with the usual chaos—plates clinking, voices rising over the hum of the ship's engine, and the occasional burst of laughter from the crew. Nana stood at the end of the long table, her heart pounding in her chest, and announced it before she could hesitate.

"I am four months with child!"

The room fell silent.

All around her, faces turned—some surprised, some grinning, some still chewing, momentarily stunned mid-bite.

Asa put down his fork. He didn't argue. He didn't ask if she was sure. He already knew.

He just looked at her-for a long moment, his dark eyes unreadable. Then, slowly, a small, knowing smile spread across his face. He reached for her hand, his fingers wrapping around hers.

"We're done, then," he said simply.

And just like that, it was decided.

The sea had been their salvation, but it would not be their future.

Chicago was not what they had expected.

The city was alive, but it wasn't the kind of life they had once known in St. Petersburg. It was louder, harsher, filled with the clash of industry—the hiss of steam, the clatter of streetcars, the distant echo of boots against pavement.

The skyline stretched high above them, black smoke curling from factory chimneys, the wind carrying the scent of iron, soot, and fresh-baked bread from the corner bakeries.

They found a small room in a crowded boarding house near the South Side, nothing more than a bed, a small table, and a stove that barely worked. The walls were thin, the pipes groaned at night, and the old woman, Maude Carson, who owned the place was strict about paying rent on time— she had no empathy, regardless. Pay up or out.

But it was land. It was solid beneath their feet.

Asa took to the streets at dawn, searching for work. Chicago was filled with men just like him—young, strong, willing—but there were too many hands and not enough jobs.

The factories were overrun with desperate workers, men standing in long lines before sunrise, waiting for a foreman to step out and pick a handful of them for a day's wages. The docks weren't any better—stevedores fought for shifts, and work was often claimed before the sun rose.

Asa knocked on doors, walked into shops, and stepped into warehouses with a quiet, steady determination. But time and time again, he came home shaking his head.

Nana did what she could, taking in mending from neighbors, stitching torn shirts, and hemming trousers for pennies. She saved every bit of food-and stretched every dollar.

She never complained.

But Asa saw the worry in her eyes when she thought he wasn't looking.

They had left the sea behind, but the land proved just as unforgiving.

Four months passed in a slow, grinding blur.

Winter crept into the city, the wind off Lake Michigan turning sharp and bitter, slicing through the streets like a knife. The cold made everything harder—the job search, the long nights, the uncertainty.

Twist of Fate

Then, one evening, just as Asa was about to turn in after another long, fruitless day, there was a knock at the door.

It wasn't a neighbor.

It wasn't someone looking for rent.

It was an opportunity.

And it would change everything.

Captain Tirone Smith, the same man who had unknowingly set their escape into motion four years earlier, had returned to Chicago.

It was unexpected, yet somehow inevitable.

He had always been a man of the sea—steady, unshaken, always moving forward. But as fate would have it, he wasn't offering them a way across the ocean this time.

He was offering them something else.

An Invitation-

They had run into him by chance.

It had been a cold afternoon, the streets of Chicago dusted with early winter frost. Asa had been on his way back from yet another dead-end job inquiry when he spotted a familiar figure standing near the docks, speaking with one of the shipping merchants.

For a moment, Asa thought he was imagining things.

But then the man turned, his rugged face breaking into a grin beneath the brim of his captain's hat.

"Well, well," Captain Smith drawled. "Look who finally found solid ground."

Asa smirked, shaking the captain's outstretched hand. "Didn't think I'd see you again."

"Didn't think I'd be back," Smith admitted. He gestured toward the city. "Chicago's got a way of pulling people in, even when they don't want it to." His eyes flicked toward Asa's worn coat, then lower, as if already guessing how things had been going.

"You and Nana making out alright?"

Asa hesitated for only a second—just long enough for Smith to see the truth.

The captain exhaled, rubbing his jaw before speaking. "Listen. I'm heading up north, back home to Traverse City." He tilted his head. "Why don't you two come with me?"

Asa frowned slightly. "To Michigan?"

Smith nodded. "Mackinaw City, first. Then, I'll be heading to my folks' place in Traverse. You two look like you could use a break."

A warm bed. A chance to rest. It was a temporary escape from the exhaustion of trying to carve out a life in a city with nothing left to offer them.

By then, Nana was nearly eight months pregnant.

She should have been hesitant. Traveling at this stage wasn't easy. But when Asa told her about the captain's offer, she didn't even pause.

"Let's go," she said simply.

Chicago had given them nothing but struggle. Maybe the answer wasn't in waiting. Maybe the answer was moving forward—again.

And so, they packed what little they owned, leaving behind the cramped boarding house, the long days of waiting in job lines, and the city streets that had grown colder with each passing week.

They followed Captain Smith north, along the coast of Lake Michigan.

The plan was simple.

Travel by boat up the Michigan coast, stop for fuel in Empire and continue toward Mackinaw City, where Captain Smith's family would be waiting.

The voyage was nothing like the ones they had taken across the Atlantic. The lake was vast but calmer, the water a deep, endless blue that stretched toward the horizon. They passed harbors dotted with fishing boats, small towns nestled against the shoreline, thick forests lining the cliffs.

At night, they anchored near the shore, the cold wind whistling through the rigging, the scent of pine and lake mist mixing with the faint smoke from the galley's stove.

It was peaceful.

For the first time in months, they weren't fighting to survive. They were simply moving forward.

Asa stood at the bow most nights, hands in his pockets, watching the water shift beneath the boat. Nana would sit nearby, leaning against a wooden crate, one hand resting against her stomach, feeling the small, steady movements of the child growing inside her.

Sometimes, Captain Smith would join them, lighting a cigar, leaning against the railing with that unreadable look in his eyes.

"You two ever think about where you want to end up?" he asked one evening.

Nana glanced at Asa. "Somewhere quiet," she murmured.

Smith chuckled, exhaling smoke. "The world ain't quiet, girl." He tilted his head toward the shore. "But up here, it gets close."

She smiled faintly. She wasn't sure if it was the answer she was looking for—but she liked the thought of it.

They reached Empire, Michigan, on a crisp autumn afternoon.

It was a tiny town with only a few homes scattered along the shore with a Sawmill and a small dock where they planned to refuel.

Captain Smith had family, Derrick Hatcher and Samantha McLaughlin-Hatcher, who lived in a century old Irish style whitewashed cottage is nestled amongst lush greenery against a backdrop of a hazy, blue-tinged sky, and some 600 feet off shoreline of Lake Michigan.

"It'll be warmer than the boat," simply said the Captain.

Both retired, Samantha and Derrick were government workers for the Department of Agriculture (USDA), who in their young teens also worked in Captain Smith parent's grocery as well as would babysit Tirone.

The cottage house was small but sturdy, made of thick stone and logs, including those painted red doors which were to ward off ghosts and evil spirits. Once inside, the sounds of the crackling fireplace in the corner gave off the sense of comfort and relaxation. The air also smelled of

"Irish Cottage by the Lake"

fresh bread and cedar, and the warmth of the place seeped into Nana's bones the second she stepped inside.

"Welcome to our home Maggie," said Samantha. "I see that glow of motherhood in the future?"

"Yes, Samantha and thank you for inviting Asa and myself," said Nana.

"Always," quipped together by both Samantha and Derrick.

"Nice to see you once again Tirone," said Samantha.

"I understand it Auntie Sammy. No need to tell me it has been a while since my last diaper change," comically expressed Tirone.

The roar of laughter rang seemed to bounce off the walls and ceiling.

"So Derrick, your home is a jewel and especially all its surroundings," said Asa.

"I agree Derrick. It is our Heaven on Earth. We purchased it from Tirone's parents, who inherited from Elizabeth's first cousins, Jacques and Catherine Bonnet-Dubois of Frankfort," he said.

When the Hatchers were doing some updates to the cottage, they found in the walls pay vouchers of Bernard Dubois who served in the American Revolutionary War in

1775, and a bill of sale of this land to him.

"See that collage of documents in that framed picture," said Samantha.

"We put that together for Tirone to remind him of his ancestral roots. When we depart the Earth, the home returns to the Moreau-Dubois next generation."

Soup's On

"I trust you're all hungry? It's been simmering all day. One of my favorite meals on these chilly fall days," said Samantha.

"Mine too!" said Derrick robustly.

"I second that," added Asa. "I could smell it before I even walked in. Brought back memories of my days on the ship—especially during those stormy times at sea." He paused, his tone shifting. "I wonder what Ellis is doing?"

"He's still with me," Tirone continued. "Tells me he'll stay forever. And if I take on any new ship assignments, he says he'll follow."

"The table is all set. Come, let us eat," said Samantha merrily.

They gathered around the table in front of the kitchen fireplace, where the soup pot hovered gently over the fire.

"Is there anything I can do to help?" Maggie asked.

"No, honey. Just sit. Munch on some of the veggies and fruits from my garden while I dish up some of this chicken soup. Pass your bowls, please," Samantha said, ladle in hand. "Derrick knows — and Tirone especially — that when I'm in my kitchen, I'm the captain of my ship. But thank you for asking, Maggie."

Laid out family-style, a platter of fresh vegetables and baskets of homemade rolls and crackers lined the center of the table.

"This soup is divine," said Maggie after her first spoonful.

Samantha smiled. "It's my grandmother's recipe. She taught me how to make it. She also taught me how to grow a garden."

Tears started to stream down Maggie's face.

"Are you okay?" Samantha asked gently.

"I'm just fine. What you said brought back such treasured memories of my Grandmother Rebecca... on her farm in St. Petersburg," Maggie replied, voice trembling.

As Derrick looked around the table, he saw the emotion mirrored in Samantha's and Asa's eyes.

He raised his glass. "Cheers, everyone. A toast to

treasured memories," he said, his voice hearty and warm.

"What's for dessert?" Derrick asked, nudging Samantha with a grin.

"It's a surprise. You've never had it," she replied with a playful smile. "It'll be ready in half an hour. Put a log on the fire in the living room—we're having it there."

"May I help you with anything, Samantha?" asked Maggie.

As the two women tidied the kitchen, the men stepped outside. Derrick had something to show Tirone in the old barn.

In the attic, a section had been turned into a small room. The walls were insulated with straw, mud, and thin wooden planks—many repurposed from old shipping crates, their faded logos still visible: *Maine Lobster and Seafood Company, New England Vegetable and Fruit Farms.*

Stuffed into the walls were pay vouchers made out to a Frederick Johnson, whose name also appeared in documents they had also found in the cottage for Bernard Dubois. Some dated back to the Revolutionary War, around 1775.

"I also found some Irish and English whiskey bottles—empty, of course. But I brought one of my own. Here, take a swig," Derrick said with a laugh.

"Johnson was my great-great-great-grandfather," he added.

Tirone's eyebrows rose. "That means we're related? I wonder where we fit in the bloodline."

"That'll take time to figure out," said Derrick. "But I do know Frederick wasn't the only male child who made it to America. They settled on the East Coast. That's where I grew up."

"How'd you end up in Michigan? What about Samantha?" Tirone asked.

"Well, long story short—because dessert's almost ready—one of my grandfathers ended up in Indianapolis. My dad moved to Traverse City. That's all I know. After college, I moved to D.C.—and that's where I met Samantha. She tells me she has Hoosier roots too."

"You've opened a can of worms," said Tirone. "I need to know more. My partner David is a professor at the *University of Mississippi*. He can help. And our son and daughter want to learn more about their heritage too."

Asa, standing nearby, looked surprised. He hadn't known about Tirone's personal life.

"It looks like we all have some discovering to do," Asa said quietly. "About our ancestors—and ourselves."

"Agreed," said Tirone. "I'll get back to you both with more details for David's research."

Just then, the sound of a bell rang out.

"That's Samantha," Derrick grinned. "Let's go see what she made."

"Right on!" Asa and Tirone bellowed in unison. "And the fifth is empty too!"

Their laughter echoed through the trees as they

made their way back to the house.

On the porch, Samantha and Maggie were enjoying the crisp night air. They looked at each other and smiled.

"They had a good time—I can tell. And I can smell it, too," said Samantha. "They'll sleep soundly... though we might not."

"I have hot brewed chamomile tea with cinnamon and honey, and one of my grandmother's special desserts— apple tarts," she added brightly.

When Asa and Maggie were at sea aboard *Freedom's Destiny*, they had once docked in Copenhagen to take on goods destined for China. With a few hours of shore leave, Asa bartered for two apple tarts. When Maggie took a bite, it brought her right back to her grandmother's kitchen in St. Petersburg and yearning for home. Maggie told Asa he should have gotten more, but had only enough money for two. He figured she would eat his also. She did.

Derrick, Tirone and Samantha were unaware of the 'tart issue' between Asa and Maggie.

"Yummy on the tarts, Samantha. Can't wait to taste one," said Asa.

"Be quiet, Asa—you offered yours to me," Maggie teased.

Everyone sat quietly as they enjoyed Samantha's

creation. Smiles replaced words. The crackling fire warmed them, inside and out.

"Anyone want more?" Samantha asked softly. "My grandmother, Nora Belle Hoffmann, used to say, '*Oh darling, you are my little princess. Come sit here, tell me how you are. Now enjoy another.*'"

"We're all fine, I think," Derrick said, pushing back from the table. "Time for me to hit the sack. How about you, Tirone? Asa? Maggie?"

All nodded in agreement.

Samantha stood. "Thank you all for offering to help clean up, but this is my quiet time. Derrick knows my ways. Please—go get ready for bed, and baste in happy thoughts."

Everyone expressed their gratitude and headed off to their rooms.

"Wait!" Samantha called. "Please take a glass of water. The air gets dry."

As Maggie passed, she gently took Samantha's hands. "I know I've been blessed, having you come into my life. Our grandmothers were so much alike."

"Yes... I felt it too," Samantha said. "I have something for you—a quilt made by my Nana Nora. It's a scene of a woman and child working in a garden. I have many of her quilts, including one just like it. No need to say anything. It's already on your bed. May it bring you comfort and more happy memories."

They embraced, holding each other tightly before going their separate ways for the night.

That evening, Nana had no idea how much she would need that warmth.

But that night, something changed.

She woke suddenly, the darkness pressing in around her, a deep, dull ache blooming in her lower back. At first, she thought it was just discomfort from all the traveling.

But then the pain came again—stronger.

She sat up, her breath hitching, one hand pressing against her belly. Too soon.

"Asa," she whispered urgently, shaking his shoulder. "Wake up."

He stirred, blinking blearily. "What's wrong?"

Another sharp pain shot through her, and she barely swallowed the gasp.

His expression changed instantly. "Is it—?"

She nodded.

Asa was out of bed in an instant, pulling on his boots and rushing to wake the captain. Despite his usual calm, Smith swore under his breath the second he understood what was happening.

The plan had been to reach Mackinaw City before the baby came.

But plans didn't matter now.

There would be no traveling north. No reaching Smith's family before Nana gave birth.

They were staying in the Empire—whether they had meant to or not.

Nathan had told this story a thousand times, each retelling etched into memory, woven into the fabric of their family's history.

"And the rest is history," he would always say, smirking, as if the whole thing had been some small, unremarkable event.

But I never tired of hearing it.

Because that single, unexpected stop in Empire— that moment when history decided for them—set the course for everything that followed.

Triumph dances with Tragedy

Weeks later, the Hatchers took their monthly outing

to Traverse City. Their first stop was always the home of Elizabeth and Edward Smith. Samantha coined this morning meal a "Parisian-Full Monty," which consisted of a delightful mix of French and English foods.

"I have made Shirred Eggs and French Toast," said Elizabeth.

Edward quipped, "What about the bacon and sausages?"

"Yes, Edward. I know you're British. Just for you, savor the fried tomatoes and mushrooms along with the Black Pudding," Elizabeth replied softly.

Their conversations were natural and effortless, flowing with an engaging exchange of ideas among the four of them. But today was somewhat different — the Hatchers were seeking advice on how they could help Asa and Maggie Grabowsky.

When Tirone finally arrived in Mackinaw City, he excitedly told his parents about his time with the Hatchers at Empire and shared the news of Maggie's recent birth to son Nathan just a month earlier. He assured the new parents that he would be back, and in the meantime, the Hatchers enthusiastically welcomed them to stay until Maggie was strong enough to return to Chicago.

"I just loved it!" said Samantha. "Our home was filled with the sounds of new life. Maggie had a glow that lit

up the entire house, and Derrick told me he could see it in me. I was able to cook up a storm using all my grandmother's recipes."

"It was sort of sad to see them go," Derrick added. "Asa helped me a lot with getting the barn in better shape, and we had many great sailing adventures on the lake."

The Smiths assured Tirone that everything would be taken care of, though he still had to work. *Freedom's Destiny* had eventually been dry-docked — something that didn't bother him too much considering his new status as a father. He became the captain of the *Prince of Tide*, a cruise ship that sailed the same routes as 'Freedom.'

"In a few months, Tirone will be bringing my grandchildren to stay with us," Elizabeth said. "David is also coming. He's taking a sabbatical from the university for needed R&R and will be working on our ancestral histories."

Samantha knew Tirone had two biological children: a son named Gregory Anthony and a daughter named Monique Susan, separated in age by only nine months. The mothers had never told Tirone he was the father, even though he maintained a relationship with both during the first two years while the *Prince of Tide* sailed to various destinations, from Duluth, Minnesota, to New Orleans.

He met Gregory's mother, Kimberly Byrne, during a tour of the *Glensheen Mansion*, where she worked as a curator. Her ancestors had emigrated from Ireland to Winnipeg, Canada, where *Freedom's Destiny* stopped.

They were a striking couple: she was tall with strawberry blonde hair, facial freckles, and mysterious green eyes. Tirone, who was a decade older, had the appearance of Clark Gable and the entrepreneurial spirit of Ted Turner. They matched like a framed Edward Hopper painting.

Monique's mother, Josephine Dupont, was the curator of European art at the *Louisiana Museum of Art* and a devout Catholic with mixed French and African ancestry.

"Josie had a combined look of a Diahann Carroll and Vivian Dandridge. A striking beauty, oozed with elegance, sophisticated style in her walk, but behind all that was fire and ice," said Tirone as he wiped his brow.

She and Tirone were drawn together during Mardi Gras, which begins 12 days before Christmas and lasts until Fat Tuesday — the day before Ash Wednesday — a time when both were grappling with their beliefs and the acceptance of their chosen life partners. Mardi Gras was the event, and New Orleans was the place to let it all out and celebrate their choices.

Initially, Tirone kept in touch with Kimberly and "Josie" through postcards, phone calls and in person whenever the ship docked in their area. However, over time, their relationship became more professional as Tirone took on new tour routes to Mexico and along the California coast, limiting their physical contact for months.

During the first two years of his children's lives, their father was known to them only by name on their birth certificates and his grandparents' address. The mothers were professional women who chose to raise their children alone without a father's daily presence or financial support, but named Tirone Smith so that when the time came for the children to know, the records would name him.

It wasn't that Kimberly or Josie didn't want to tell Tirone; they simply didn't want to tie down a man for their choice to have children. Their physical encounters were not meant to resemble a honeymoon night or the consummation of marriage, but rather represented a chosen passion that brought their children to life through a man blessed with strong morals and a lineage rich with compassion for all who defied the odds during difficult times.

Both women understood that unforeseen circumstances should be addressed in case something happened to them, leaving the children without a biological parent. Though they had their maternal grandparents, they recognized the importance of fraternal connections. They had met Tirone's parents during tours of the Prince of Tide and found them to embody the same characteristics of respect, honesty, responsibility, and commitment to family.

While touring the West Coast, Tirone met David

Price for the first time aboard a yacht that catered to passengers during one of those wine-tasting tours. Over several days, they made stops at Fisherman's Wharf, Alcatraz Island, the Golden Gate Bridge, and other notable sites. David, who was on loan from the *University of Mississippi* to lecture at the *University of San Francisco* on family history and ancestry, initiated a conversation when he spotted Tirone sporting an "Ole Miss" ballcap and T-shirt.

"I see you're a fan of my university," David quipped, with his perfectly liberal and outgoing personality.

"I sure am! Been one for several years since I left sailing the oceans and took to the rivers," Tirone replied.

As time went on, they kept in touch regularly while Tirone continued his tours on the West Coast. However, when he returned to the Mississippi River, primarily for day trips, David went back to his teaching role at the university. Their relationship blossomed into a life partnership that culminated in a legal marriage of equality, *"to have and to hold from this day forward, for better, for worse, for richer, for poorer until death do us part,"* with no strings attached.

It has been said that triumph often dances with tragedy. Yet this time, what had been shielded from Tirone became a stark reality: instant fatherhood to a son and daughter, barely three years old.

Within days of each other, Kimberly lost her life in a plane crash en route to Aruba, where she was set to curate works by Agnès van Vliet, Anita Hugen, Annet van Doorm, Carlos Rojas, and Danilo Geerman at the Archaeological Museum, as well as various works at the Museum of Industry and Fort Zoutman Historical Museum. The assignment was set to last 45 days.

Josie's passing was much different; she and her male companion were on a tour of Mexico when they were abducted by a radical gang known for racial violence. They were never found, and the case was eventually closed.

The maternal grandparents upheld their daughters' last wills and testaments, contacting Tirone and presenting him with all documents proving he was the children's father. Each mother had written a letter, sealed and meant to be opened only by Tirone, requesting his consideration to raise their children. There was no hesitation on his or David's part—they were eager to adopt.

"The letters were delivered to us by their attorneys. Edward and I were permitted to open and read them since Tirone was on tour," said Elizabeth. "I was overwhelmed by the news, but felt my prayers were answered."

"Mom couldn't reach me; only David she could. He let me know, and to say I was shocked would be an understatement. I contacted my boss to inform him I had to return home for an urgent family matter," said Tirone.

Days after the notifications, both sets of the children's maternal grandparents brought them to the Smith home in Traverse City.

"Will you be able to stay with us and the children? I want them to know you will always be in their lives," Tirone added. "I know they are very young and may not understand, but please visit as often as you can, and I will make sure they visit you."

All agreed, and for the next two weeks, both sets of grandparents basked in their newfound joy.

Back to the Windy, Baby in Hand

The winter in Chicago was harsh, Lake Michigan's icy winds slicing through the streets, chilling them to the bone. Nana and Asa had arrived with their newborn son, a city full of possibility stretched before them—but in 1939, the possibility wasn't enough to survive.

The Great Depression had officially ended, but its scars still lingered. Factories were running again, but not fast enough to provide work for every man lining up at the doors. The steel mills along the Calumet River roared back to life, but only for those lucky enough to be chosen in the morning crowds of desperate workers.

Once the beating heart of the city's labor force, the

stockyards on the South Side still reeked of blood and sweat, but even there, jobs were scarce. Men gathered outside the plants before dawn, waiting, hoping. Asa was among them for a time, waking early-and joining the line, but coming home just as often empty-handed.

Meanwhile, Nana did what she could. The boarding house they lived in was cramped, filled with immigrants like them—men and women who had come with dreams and now fought for survival. She took in sewing work, patched clothes, and stretched every meal until it could be stretched no more.

But Chicago was ruthless.

They had left the endless, shifting sea behind, but now they faced a different kind of uncertainty—the kind that came with hunger, a baby who needed more than they could give, and nights spent wondering if they had made the right choice.

Then, Captain Smith returned.

It had been months since they had last seen him, and yet, when he walked through the door of their small rented room, it was as if no time had passed.

"You two look like hell," he remarked dryly, arms crossed over his chest. "I told you I would be back. Congratulate me, I became a father of a son and daughter. I will fill you in later," said Tirone.

Asa exhaled, shaking his head. "Chicago's not what we thought."

Smith nodded. "Never is." He leaned against the wall, eyes flicking toward Nana, who was rocking their son Nathan in her arms, exhaustion clear in her features.

Then, just as simply as he had once offered them passage across the sea, he made another offer.

"My folks in Traverse City are getting on in years," he said. "They own a store. They need help running it."

Asa blinked. "A store?"

Smith shrugged. "It's steady work. Steady pay. And hell, it's quieter than this." He gestured vaguely to the thin walls, to the city beyond them, always buzzing, always moving, never stopping.

Nana looked up at Asa. He didn't have to ask. She already knew the answer.

Chicago had given them nothing but struggle. Maybe their future wasn't here.

Maybe it was somewhere quieter.

Somewhere like Traverse City.

They arrived in Northern Michigan in the early spring of 1940.

Traverse City was nothing like Chicago. No towering buildings, no factories billowing smoke, no lines of men waiting for work. Instead, it was a place of rolling cherry orchards, dense forests, and the endless blue stretch of Grand Traverse Bay.

"Waldoboro, Maine Market"

Elizabeth and Edward Smith's grocery store sat on a busy street in town, its wooden sign faded but welcoming. The bell above the door jingled as customers came and went, the smell of fresh bread mixing with the scent of old wood and ground coffee.

Asa took to the work quickly—stocking shelves, handling shipments, and managing accounts. He had spent years hauling cargo on ships; now, he was hauling crates of canned goods and bags of flour.

Nana worked behind the counter, greeting customers, learning the ins and outs of keeping the books, handling the register, and making small talk with the regulars.

They were still young—too young, maybe, to be running a business—but Elizabeth saw something in them, the same resilience that had brought her across an ocean so many years before.

"You remind me of myself," Elizabeth told Nana one evening, watching as she balanced her son on one hip while counting coins in the till. "Starting over in a place you never expected."

Nana smiled tiredly. "Did you ever regret it?"

Elizabeth shook her head. "No." Then, softer, "And neither will you."

The early years were not easy, but they were steady.

The store became their livelihood, their foundation. It was where they spent their days, where Asa's hands grew calloused from unloading deliveries, where Nana found herself trading stories with the local women, building friendships that made her feel—for the first time in years—like she belonged.

Nathan, who was born in the winter of '39, his cries filling the small house behind the store, his tiny hands clutching at his mother's fingers as if he already knew how much strength it had taken for her to bring him into the world.

Asa held him gently, his son, his future, the proof that they had built something real, something lasting.

Nathan grew stronger, toddling through the aisles, watching his father work, and listening to his mother sing softly as she stocked shelves.

He would grow up here.

Not in Russia. Not on a ship.

But in Traverse City, in the place they had never planned to be but had somehow, against all odds, found themselves calling home.

But life, as always, was unpredictable.

Their second child was lost before he ever took his first breath.

It was winter, the cold creeping in through the cracks in the walls, the weight of exhaustion pressing against Nana's chest. She had felt the pain first in the early hours of the morning, sharp and undeniable. By the time the doctor arrived, it was already over.

She had lost a child before—on the journey from Russia, during the years at sea—but this was different. This was a loss that came when they had finally thought they were safe.

She didn't speak of it often after that. But she carried it with her, always.

And then, as if to remind them that life never stops

moving, she was with child again, but Nathan became Asa and Nana's only living creation.

Five years after arriving, the Smiths—Elizabeth and Edward, now aging, ready to step away from the long hours and the demands of running a store—made them an offer.

"The store should go to you," Elizabeth said simply. And it did.

The young couple who had once been drifters, who had once moved with the tide, now had roots.

Nana and Asa had come to America without a home, without a plan, without certainty.

But now, without ever intending to, they had found the place they were meant to be.

Because sometimes, the journey isn't about where you plan to go—sometimes, the journey is about where you end up—when fate decides you're home.

"Blessing from Above"

A NEW LEGACY BEGINS TO UNFOLD

*"What sunshine is to flowers, smiles are to humanity. These are but trifles, to be sure;
but scattered along life's pathway, the good they do is inconceivable."*
Joseph Addison [05-01-1672-6-17-1719]

♥

Culturally, Tirone Smith embodies a blend of French and English heritage. His parents immigrated from Europe to escape the looming shadows of political and social unrest, as well as the devastation brought on by World War I in the early 1900s. They sought refuge in America, a land celebrated for its freedoms—life, liberty, and the pursuit of happiness.

In many ways, Tirone was a privileged child. As an only child, he enjoyed more opportunities than most, including music and art lessons, and was provided with better clothing. However, he was also expected to earn these privileges by contributing to numerous household chores. While he did not live in luxury, the true riches that his parents, Elizabeth and Edward Smith, instilled within him were a sense of responsibility for his actions, respect for authority, and an appreciation for religious and cultural traditions. These values ultimately guided him to his first major leadership role as the captain of *Freedom's Destiny*, his "lifeboat" of endless experiences. This position exposed him to diverse peoples and communities around the world, each with unique lifestyles, languages, and strong ties to their ancestral lands and resources.

Had Tirone possessed what Benjamin enjoyed—a treasured grandparent who engaged in divination—perhaps signs would have foretold a life dedicated to serving humankind, infused with a deep empathy aimed at elevating others to their rightful place on Earth. Evidence of such a calling was already visible in his leadership of a vessel that traveled the globe, his involvement with those who served aboard, and in his intuitive guidance, as if steered by unseen hands. This guidance propelled his growth in caring for Asa and Maggie Grabowsky, as well as in addressing the needs of his aging parents. It extended even to the women who chose him as a partner to fulfill their desires, unknowingly connected to a mother's wish and resulting in the creation of a new generation.

From his Mardi Gras days, where he and Josie battled the demons of societal acceptance and religious norms, to his time commanding the *Prince of Tide* on the West Coast, Tirone sought a connection with David—a quest he had been engaged in since his teenage years. This connection rekindled feelings for his late friend, Johnny Johnson, who had tragically drowned, plunging Tirone into unbearable sorrow. This loss was not rooted in physical attraction but rather in a bond akin to the love a son holds for a father or sibling. He ultimately discovered that his relationship with David alleviated the aches brought on by societal expectations, allowing his internal struggles to cease as he embraced his new role as a father.

Young children require a combination of emotional, social, and physical support to thrive—nurturing care, love, and guidance from their parents. Tirone and David fully embraced their new roles without hesitation regarding their own careers. However, many others had paved the way for the new generation to settle in without worry.

The maternal grandparents, Carter and Ava Freedman-Dupont, and the paternal grandparents, Edward and Elizabeth-Moreau-Smith, along with Aunt Samantha and Uncle Derrick McLaughlin-Hatcher, provided built-in caregiving, empowering Tirone and David with the emotional strength needed to handle their transition and career changes from their home in Oxford, Mississippi, to Traverse City, Michigan. During this adjustment period, they raised their children, Greggory Anthony and Monique Susan Smith, in a worry-free environment.

The Smiths resided in the Boardman Neighborhood in a grand Victorian-style home. This house had been constructed by a former lumber business owner who thoughtfully designed a separate wing for her parents, granting them independence and the freedom to come and go. Upon moving in, the Smiths occupied this wing as their primary living quarters, as it included two baths and two bedrooms, making it feel like a single-family home. As

Tirone matured, he was given the option to move to the main section on the second floor, which featured an ensuite bath and five additional bedrooms serviced by one bath.

Elizabeth converted one bedroom into a den for Tirone's homework, pictures, mementos, toys, and a space for him and his friends to socialize. Other bedrooms served guests, including Aunt Samantha and Uncle Derrick during their caregiving visits.

"Mom was extra happy when I moved upstairs. She always told me not to be concerned about making too much noise," Tirone recalled.

David interjected, "My mother told me, 'A house needs to grow, and sounds are its food.'"

The grandparents eagerly wanted to fill all six bedrooms, but health conditions challenged this until Tirone, David, and their children took up residency. The grandparents, needless to say, were overjoyed.

"I am fulfilled," Tirone declared.

"Might I add, becoming a dad puts me simply in my glory!" David chimed in.

"Amens" filled the living room air.

With Asa and Maggie now owning the store, and the new fathers navigating the chaos of child-rearing, the grandparents found time to travel and enjoy uninterrupted sessions with David as he delved into family histories.

His research began not only with Elizabeth but also with her first cousin, Jacques Dubois, and his wife, Catherine, whom she stayed with when she emigrated to America. Derrick Hatcher uncovered militia and other documents dating back to the War of 1775 for Bernard Dubois, and the house gifted to Elizabeth by Jacques. He discovered pay vouchers for Frederick Johnson, with whom he shares family history ties, along with wooden planks used for wall coverings, emblazoned with faded logos for *Maine Lobster and Seafood Company* and *New England Vegetable and Fruit Farms.*

David's research indicates that Frederick Johnson and Bernard Dubois served in the British and French armies. Despite their distaste for monarchies and aristocracies, they were swept into the military and found themselves on American soil.

Upon the war's end in September 1783, Frederick and Bernard defected from their regimes and embarked on a journey north to Canada. Their paths first crossed in Portland, Maine, where the harsh winter weather stalled further travel. Luckily, they managed to eke out a living in the lumber industry, which provided for their basic needs as they awaited spring to continue their northern journey. Records indicate they never reached Canada; they ended up in Calais and Eastport, Maine, due to devastating hurricanes and flooding.

Still feeling the war's effects, both men were weary and worn from strenuous labor in the lumber industry; this marked the beginning of their American roots in Washington County, known as "Sunrise County," where the sun first rises in the United States, named after George Washington.

These young immigrants from England and France were ultimately captivated by American feminine love, producing numerous sons and daughters.

"In my further digging, I found that the Dubois and Johnson extended relatives encompass a population of almost half of Calais, around three thousand," David revealed. "I also discovered amusing entries by Joseph Johnson regarding them."

One entry notes, "*Frederick and Bernard were quite the attraction when engaged in discussions about freedoms. It was often when they were in their rebellious moods, especially after too much Irish whiskey…*"

Another, "*Frederick's upper-class English accent clashed with Bernard's French rolling of the 'R's,' as each took individual righteous stances on any subject. Yet only a keen heart could see through their bravado. They were best friends, and no fists would ever fly. They provided the night's entertainment at Waldo's, the local pub.*"

Where Elizabeth and Derrick fit into these ancestral trees remains unresolved. However, in David's preliminary

summary, he suggests:

1. Jacques Dubois is the first generation to arrive in America in 1908, possibly to escape the looming threat of

war and political and social divisions. At nearly 30, no family records before him are known. His father, Louis Dubois, was the brother of Elizabeth's father, Pierre Dubois.

2. Derrick Hatcher's connection with Frederick Johnson leads to the assumption that his roots are maternal, as records show a daughter married a Hatcher from East Pointe, Maine.

Tirone reminded David of something Derrick had said during a visit to his home in Empire about the peculiar connections he found while visiting farmers in the field. They all seemed linked, either by family or friends.

"All this ancestry stuff reminds me of 'six degrees of separation' — how any two people on Earth can be connected through a chain of no more than six acquaintances," Tirone mused.

"It hasn't been proven. But if it is true, I'd have a solid chance of winning if I were to run for national political office, given my years in teaching!" David quipped.

"Ha! How do you suppose that, Professor Price? Maybe most of your students couldn't stand you and only took your course to graduate," Tirone chuckled.

"Be quiet, Smith! Go take Gregory's sailboats and play with them in the tub," David retorted, grinning.

With a new month approaching, it was time for the Hatcher outing to the Smiths, but this year it would take place at the Smith home instead of the store. Initially, Elizabeth and Samantha had named the new occasion *"Once Upon a Saturday,"* but in the coming months, it evolved into *"A Weekend of Wonders,"* beginning again with their cherished French and English breakfasts. Elizabeth was determined to uphold the traditions she had with Derrick and Samantha; they were her American family.

Both Elizabeth and Edward felt the joy one experiences when families reunite during holidays. Though decades had passed, they never forgot their youthful years in their birth countries. Both were eager, particularly Samantha, who looked forward to testing more of her grandmother's recipes and baking apple tarts for the Grabowskys.

Derrick had been in touch with David regarding some discoveries in the barn's attic. "I'll bring them on Saturday," he said.

The weekend arrived, with Elizabeth preparing breakfast. Edward and Tirone popped in for coffee. "Cooking up a storm, I see, my sweet!" Edward exclaimed.

"Just doing what brings me joy, and you know how your tummy loves it!" Elizabeth replied cheerfully.

Samantha was in her playful Auntie Sammy mood, entertaining Gregory and Monique. Derrick and David discussed ancestral history, while Tirone and Edward retreated to the front porch with their morning coffee. The neighborhood buzzed with the arrival of families; children piled out of cars, racing up and down sidewalks, while mothers shouted for them to come back for a meal.

"It hasn't changed in all these years, Dad," Tirone observed.

"There's only one exception—you're no longer one of those kids I see running about," Edward replied nostalgically. "I can picture you and your best buddy, Johnny, racing each other." Tirone's eyes swelled with emotion. To stave off his feelings, he stood, cleared his throat, and firmly declared, "Mom is ringing the bell. Samantha is warning us that it's time to eat. Shall we go, Dad?"

As the day wore on, the family split up to engage in different activities, together and alone. Elizabeth and Samantha ventured into town to shop and lunch at their favored spot, Mabel's. Derrick and David went to the marina where Edward docked his boat; all three enjoyed a leisurely cruise around the lake combined with a bit of fishing.

"I caught one! Me too!" declared David and Derrick in unison. From there, they ventured for food and drinks at Randy's, a rustic bar tucked off the beaten path on the lake. Tirone stayed home to attend to the children's needs— feeding schedules, diaper changes, playtime, and naps.

Saturday evening meals took place in their kitchen,

where they all gathered at the large round table. Elizabeth had a special name for this meal: "*A Little of This and That.*" Edward joked, "You mean leftovers?" Tirone and David, who were just setting the children in their high chairs, were within earshot of their conversation.

"No, Mr. Smith! I'm sure many remnants from the week's finest meals found their way into your Westinghouse," Elizabeth replied with a smile. "When Tirone was younger, I'd have him invite friends over for Saturday lunches, and they'd all agree, especially Johnny, that it was like attending one of those outdoor food festivals. And you, Mr. Smith, can look forward to several exceptional beers like Mackesons and Guinness to savor!"

"Enough said, I got it," Edward responded.

Johnny's name had now surfaced twice during the day, stirring emotions within Tirone. David, attuned to Tirone's past with Johnny, sensed that it would evoke tears, and this was a time for celebration.

To divert Tirone's thoughts, David boldly declared to Elizabeth, "This and That has now become a Price tradition." Turning to Tirone, he asked, "What do you think of that, Mr. Smith?" Tirone extended his hand for a shake, nodding his approval.

As evening approached, the family gathered in the living room of the main house. Asa, Maggie, and Nathan joined, regulars for socializing. A spread of sweets, crafted by Samantha and Elizabeth from their grandmother's recipes, adorned the buffet.

David excitedly dumped a box of toys onto the floor, which included teddy bears, Lincoln logs, matchbox cars, and more noise-making contraptions for the children. Giggles, chatter, and wind-up sounds filled the air, bringing smiles to the tots' faces.

"How about some music, Edward? I'd love to hear Frank Sinatra while sipping on a Pink Squirrel you'll make for me and Maggie," Elizabeth proposed.

"You got it, my sweet," Edward replied.

"Hey Dad, while you're behind the bar, I'll take a Tom Collins, heavy on the gin," Tirone added. "Samantha will have a Golden Cadillac, Derrick wants a Grasshopper, and if you've got any more of that Russian Vodka, whip up one of your signatures for Asa," Tirone said cheerfully. "I'll be right back," Derrick announced, heading off to retrieve the discoveries from the barn's attic.

Once the treasures were spread across the coffee table, a bill of sale for "bleuets" was revealed. "That's French for blueberries," David explained.

Additionally, unwrapped from crumbling paper was a small cloth pouch containing three round wooden objects, each the size of a checker, adorned with markings. He handed them to David for examination, eager for answers.

"Well, the writing is all in French; 'payé' means 'paid' in English, and it's signed by Bernard Dubois," David noted.

"What about the wooden pieces?" Derrick inquired. "They appear part of a board game. The symbols on them are Greek to me, but the words beneath read: *Wealth, Gift,* and *Lake,*" Derrick observed.

"Come to think of it, I saw these before. I faintly recall playing with them as a child. In my teens, I noticed my mother wore a necklace sporting similar symbols. Long story short, she claimed it was an heirloom passed down from mother to daughter," Derrick explained.

The newfound treasures sparked memories for Elizabeth and Maggie, drawing parallels with their own experiences. One marked *"Wealth"* resembled the letter F; another stamped *"Lake"* looked like an upside-down checkmark, while the last marked *"Gift"* resembled an X. The two women agreed they resembled Rune Stones, traditionally used for guidance or answers.

"My dad always carried the *Wealth* piece in his vest pocket," Maggie shared. "He said it was merely a family memento, one his father received from his father."

"I've never encountered those wooden pieces, but my grandmother, Rebecca, made clothes that embodied symbols, like the X, Star of David, and others. My dad adored the fur hat she made," Elizabeth reminisced.

What remains to unfold in this ancestral research is that Frederick Johnson was the founder of the *Maine Lobster and Seafood Company*, while Bernard Dubois established *New England Vegetable and Fruit Farms*. The question of how or why they ended up in Traverse City, Michigan, lingers ominously. Could it merely be business? After all, Traverse City is renowned as the *'Cherry Capital of the World'* and hosted its first National Cherry Festival in 1925. Might it also relate to Michigan's esteemed diversity in fish populations, including walleye, northern pike, and smallmouth bass?

For months, Professor David Price meticulously pored over records, hidden family letters, and forgotten diaries in search of the Dubois-Johnson ancestry and the elusive Hatcher connection. The town's whispered gossip traced his lineage back to the enigmatic Dubois-Johnson family—figures who danced between history and myth. They were a family both notorious and revered, entangled in triumphs and struggles, bound by an unsolved mystery that had plagued the town for generations.

What drove Elizabeth to abandon her foreign roots? Was it simply the war, or was she, perhaps, a chosen vessel guided by the souls of her ancestors in America, instructed to build upon their beginnings? The children she lost—were they not merely gone but transformed, their spirits reborn through the seed of her son, Tirone? What essence of destiny lay within him, waiting to be unveiled?

And then there's Maggie. The delicate embroidery of the Star of David and the Gift Rune on her clothes—were these merely decorative heirlooms crafted by her grandmother, or did they harbor secrets of a preordained path? Was she the chosen one, destined to forge roots in America for her Jewish ancestors, provided with a vision to see into the unknown future?

As the sun dipped below the horizon, casting a warm golden hue across the quiet town of Empire, Derrick stood at the edge of the lake, looking back at the old barn. The trees whispered secrets in the evening breeze, their gnarled branches like spirited fingers beckoning him forward. As the last rays of light caressed the remnants of the barn, he felt an overwhelming pull—an energy that bound him to this place more profoundly than he could comprehend.

With the final light of day extinguishing itself, time will tell if the connections—be they family, friends, or foes—lead to the unveiling of the Dubois-Johnson legacy. As shadows danced on the lake's surface, a flicker of uncertainty surrounded Tirone, hinting that he might hold the key to unlocking the past—a past that waited patiently in the depths of history, ready to be revealed.

"A Long Way Home"

122

EARLY YEARS: 1947-1953

*"By means of an image we can often hold onto our lost belongings.
But it is the desperateness of losing which picks the flowers
of memory, binds the bouquet."*

French Novelist Colette

♥

The fire in the hearth cast long, flickering shadows across the walls as my father, Nathan, leaned back in his chair, a satisfied sigh escaping him. This was his element—talking about the past, about the paper, about the life that shaped him.

He took a slow sip of his coffee, the steam curling up toward his face.

"I peddled the local rag in my early elementary age years," he began, his voice thick with nostalgia. "Ran those streets like I had ink in my veins. Sold every edition before noon. Didn't matter if it was rain or snow—I had a route, and I ran it."

I smirked. "And you had a mouth on you, too."

Dad chuckled, shaking his head. "Oh, you bet. My mother used to say, 'Nathan, you could sell ink to the printers themselves.'"

He drummed his fingers against the chair's armrest.

"When I turned 13, they let me inside. Called it a promotion." He shot me a wry look. "Fancy way of saying I got to mop floors and clean the printing presses."

I raised an eyebrow. "Maintenance engineer?"

He laughed. "Damn straight! *That's* what they called it. But let me tell you, Benny, I didn't care one bit. Because I got to be inside."

His voice dropped slightly, the weight of that moment settling over him.

"The smell of fresh ink, the sound of the presses hammering out the morning's headlines — it was electric. And the reporters, Benny... they were something else." He leaned forward, eyes shining. "They didn't just write the news. They *chased* it. They lived it."

I could see it in his expression — the awe, the hunger. My father wasn't just a kid with a mop. He was a kid standing on the threshold of a world he knew he belonged to.

And then, Murray Bernard arrived.

Dad's fingers tapped against the side of his coffee cup as he looked toward the old photograph on the mantle.

"You know, Benny, the paper was going under when Bernard bought it. It was a mess — bad management, losing subscribers, barely hanging on. Nobody thought it was gonna last another year."

I picked up the photo, running my fingers over the aged frame.

Murray Bernard.

Even in the grainy black-and-white image, he had presence. Tall—over six feet—with broad shoulders and a frame that looked built for work, not just boardrooms. His silvery white hair only made him seem sharper, more defined.

His eyes were the kind that saw everything.

Dad let out a breath.

"You should've seen him walk in that first day," he murmured. "Didn't matter that he was from the East Coast. Didn't matter that he wasn't born here. The second he set foot in that office, it was *his*."

I set the photo down. "What made him buy it?"

Dad smirked. "Because Bernard didn't just see a failing newspaper. He saw something worth saving."

He leaned back, stretching his arms before settling in again.

"But to understand Murray, you gotta go back to where he came from."

Dad took another sip of coffee before continuing, his voice softer now, as if pulling the memories from the past itself.

"Murray's family didn't start with money, Benny. His grandparents — Levi Bernard and Abigail Goldberg — they were just kids when they married. Late teens. It was Vilna, Lithuania, back before the war."

I knew where this was going.

"They left?"

Dad nodded. "Not just left. Fled. They were on one of the last ships out of Hamburg before World War I."

I let that sink in.

"If they had waited even a few more months..." Dad's voice trailed off, and he shook his head. "It would've been a different story. They would've never made it."

I imagined them — two teenagers, boarding a crowded ship, carrying everything they owned in a bag no bigger than a suitcase. Not because they wanted to, but because they had to.

"They landed in New York City," Dad continued. "The Lower East Side. Like most Jewish immigrants back then, they found work where they could."

He smiled faintly.

"Levi was a tailor. Abigail, a seamstress. And damn good ones, too."

I tilted my head. "That's how they made it?"

"Yeah," Dad said. "They didn't have much, but they had their hands. And that was enough. They started small—

a little shop called *Yiddish Threads*. Sold hand-stitched clothes to the locals. Didn't take long before word got around—if you wanted real quality, you went to Bernard."

He gestured toward the photo again.

"And that's where Murray's father, Asher Samuel Bernard, came in. He was the one who turned it from a family shop into a real business. Managed the money, handled the suppliers, made sure they didn't just survive— they *grew*."

I exhaled. "So that's where Murray learned it. Not just from his dad, but from watching his grandparents build something out of nothing."

Dad nodded, his eyes flickering with something close to pride.

"Exactly."

Business in Motion

The business office at the Traverse City Post wasn't

as loud as the newsroom, but had its own kind of madness when payroll week rolled around

The steady clack-clack-clack of typewriters filled the space, interrupted by the occasional ring of the phone or the whirring churn of the printing calculator. Stacks of invoices, pay stubs, and ad contracts covered nearly every available surface.

At the center of it all sat Joanne Wieman, the Business Manager, glasses perched low on her nose, cigarette dangling from her lips, muttering to herself as she worked through a mess of numbers.

And beside her was Virginia Bernard, sleeves rolled up, fingers flipping through pages with practiced speed.

Virginia wasn't officially on staff, but when the pressure was on—especially during payroll and advertiser billing—she was always there.

Joanne huffed, typing a set of figures into her adding machine and scowling at the result.

"Damn it," she muttered, jabbing the keys again. "I swear, if these numbers don't match up, I'm throwing myself into the press."

Virginia barely glanced up. "Do that and you'll just give the typesetters a headache!"

Joanne shot her a look over her glasses. "You joke

now, but I've been in this chair since seven-thirty this morning, and the only thing keeping me from losing my mind is this cigarette and the hope that I'll drop dead before next month's payroll."

Virginia smirked, reaching over to pull a sheet from Joanne's stack. "Well, let's avoid the dying part and just get through this, shall we?"

Joanne exhaled sharply, rubbing her temples. "Murray sure knows how to run a paper, but you'd think he'd let me hire an extra set of hands for this nightmare."

Virginia gave her a pointed look. "And you'd just yell at them the whole time."

Joanne shrugged, unbothered. "That's what good training looks like."

Virginia laughed under her breath, flipping through another set of invoices. "Alright, what's missing?"

Joanne reached for a separate pile of papers, flipping through them with the speed of someone who had done this a thousand times before.

"Ad rates from the new businesses — still waiting on a final number from Simmons' Hardware, and those new boys over at the auto shop in Petoskey haven't sent their check yet."

Virginia nodded, tapping a pen against the desk. "Simmons is solid—they'll pay. The auto shop?" She exhaled through her nose. "They're still fresh, they'll probably need a reminder."

Joanne sighed dramatically. "Great. Another 'friendly' phone call where I have to listen to some man tell me how he's 'just waiting on one last payment' before he can settle his ad bill."

Virginia smirked. "You could let Murray handle it."

Joanne snorted. "Please. If he calls, the poor man will have a stroke before the conversation is over. I'll take care of it."

Virginia shook her head, a small smile playing on her lips. "Let me know if you need me to send the girls over to collect."

Joanne stopped mid-page, looking up. "Now that's an idea. Get Roberta in here—she's got her father's presence, just in a smaller frame."

Virginia smirked. "Exactly. She walks in, arms crossed, doesn't say a word, just wait for them to hand the check over. Works every time."

Joanne laughed, finally punching in the right number on the adding machine.

As much as Virginia helped in the business office, she wasn't the only Bernard making herself useful at the paper.

Bernard's daughters—Roberta, Jennifer, and Barbara—practically grew up in the building.

They knew the smell of fresh ink on newsprint before they knew the smell of cookies in an oven.

They had spent their childhood running between desks, dodging stressed-out reporters, and helping wherever they could.

The eldest, Roberta, was methodical—sharp like her mother, business-minded like her grandfather Asher.

She had a habit of standing at the business office doorway, arms crossed, scanning the room like she was already in charge.

Virginia once joked, "If you ever lose your job, Joanne, Roberta will take it before the ink dries on your resignation letter."

Roberta, only sixteen at the time, had smirked. "I'll give you a week's notice."

Joanne had nearly choked on her coffee.

Jennifer, the middle child, was a natural snoop.

She was always hanging around the newsroom,

listening in on reporters' conversations, lingering by the press machines, peeking over the typesetters' shoulders.

She had a way of absorbing information without ever asking direct questions—something that made the editors uneasy.

"Jennifer," one of them had warned her once, "if you keep eavesdropping on classified stories, we're going to have to start putting you on the payroll."

She had just grinned and responded, "I'll take it."

Barbara, the youngest, was the wild card.

She wasn't afraid of anyone. Not the editors, not the pressmen, and certainly not the advertisers who thought they could smooth-talk their way out of paying on time.

One time, she marched up to an ad salesman who had been dodging his payments for weeks and slammed a ledger on his desk.

"Pay up," she had said, hands on her hips, completely unfazed by the man twice her size.

He had laughed—until he saw Murray standing behind her, arms crossed, nodding in approval.

The check was on Virginia's desk the next morning.

Barbara's personality trait of boldness, not being shy in asking for payment from clients was a Goodwill asset

Murray admired. He told her that often and padded her allowance for a job well-done.

However, there are times when she skipped over the fine print. Her art teacher, Patrick Levy told of a time when her forward-thinking style raised many hairs. However it didn't phase him because where he grew-up and educated, New Jersey, New York City, Baltimore, Barbara brought her dog to class to serve as the subject for a live drawing assignment was not out of the ordinary, but...

"What we have here Miss Bernard?" voiced Mr. Levy.

"It's Rusty, my dog. He is my live subject to draw and paint," quipped Barbara.

"I said last week we are going to do some live-like draw subjects I will display on the easels," said Mr. Levy. "I admire your contribution to this art assignment, but this is not the place for a live subject."

Rusty starts a barking jag, turning wildly in a circle. Students become excited, frustrated, and sensitive to heighten noise. Barbara tries to console him and soon after Principal Sommers enters the art room and steps into a pool fluid Rusty made.

"What's with the pooch, Mr. Levy?" said Mr. Sommers.

"Barbara misunderstood today's art class assignment. We are doing a still-life artwork as if those on the easel were live subjects," said teacher Levy. "Barbara is taking her dog home now."

"Thanks everyone for welcoming Rusty," cheerfully expressed Barbara. In a low tone, "I will be back shortly Mr. Levy."

"Nobody got special treatment," Dad continued. "They worked just as hard as the rest of us. Hell, some days, they worked harder."

I leaned forward. "And they all stayed in the business?"

Dad nodded. "For a while. Roberta stuck with the financial side. Jennifer did a stint in journalism before finding her way into publishing. Barbara?" He laughed. "She scared off enough advertisers that she got a job in corporate sales."

I shook my head, grinning. "They weren't just a family — they were part of the machine."

Dad tapped the arm of his chair. "That's the thing, Benny. The best newspapers aren't just businesses. They're families."

And the Bernards were both.

Dad leaned forward, tapping his fingers against the

armrest as if he could still hear the rhythm of the newsroom buzzing in his mind.

"The Chief wasn't just a name on the door, Benny," he said. "He was everywhere. Every morning, like clockwork, he walked through that newsroom, stopping at every desk, checking in with everyone from the pressmen to the editors. And he never rushed through it, either. He made time. Because the paper wasn't just news to him—it was people."

Dad's voice had that particular tone I recognized— the one he used when he talked about things that truly mattered to him.

"You'd hear him before you saw him," he continued. "His boots against the tile, the jingle of the change in his pocket, the way he always cleared his throat right before he spoke."

He shook his head with a small laugh. "And every morning, like clockwork, his first stop was Esther Bierman."

Esther was impossible to miss in any room. Dressed to the hilt every day, she carried herself with the kind of confidence that made men nervous. She wasn't just the editor of the paper—she was the damn pulse of it. She had an iron grip on the news cycle and an eye for a good headline that even the Chief himself respected.

Murray leaned against the edge of her desk, flipping through the morning's drafts.

"Alright, Esther, what's keeping Traverse City awake today?"

She didn't look up, her red pencil darting across the copy with sharp, precise edits.

"Fire over on Maple and Sixth last night, Chief. Took down a bakery and a barber shop. No injuries, but the fire department had to fight it for hours."

Murray let out a long whistle, adjusting the unlit cigar between his fingers. "Damn shame about the bakery. Who doesn't love fresh bread?"

Esther finally glanced up. "Well, now we all get to love it charred."

He smirked and moved to the next column. "Stormfront moving in?"

She nodded. "Could flood the back roads. We got Simmons on it."

Murray grunted, then turned his head toward the teletype machine, which was hammering out national headlines in that steady, unrelenting rhythm. He scanned the latest printout:

STOCKS SLIDE AGAIN, FED SIGNALS POSSIBLE INTEREST RATE HIKE

He scoffed. "Jesus. Wall Street panics every time a banker bellows a sneeze."

Esther smirked. "I was gonna phrase it differently, butt-wind, but yeah."

Murray tapped the page. "Alright, keep the fire above the fold, and give the storm a strong second. But if Washington pulls any real stunts today, we might need to shift things around."

Esther nodded. "Not my first rodeo, Chief."

"Damn right it isn't," Murray said, tapping his cigar against her desk before walking on.

He made his way to Ruth Ann Dunkin, the paper's City Hall reporter. She had already dug herself into a pile of legal documents, flipping through her notes like she was preparing to take the mayor himself to trial.

You could always tell when Ruth Ann was in the building. Before you even saw her, you'd catch a whiff of her rose perfume, the scent lingering in the air like a signature. And then, of course, there was her voice—sultry, low, like she should've been announcing jazz records on late-night radio instead of covering zoning ordinances.

Murray pulled up a chair and leaned in. "Alright, Ruthie. What's the city up to today? Fixing roads or stealing wallets?"

She didn't even blink. "Water rates are going up five percent. City Council voted on it last night, buried the discussion under some fluff about 'infrastructure improvements.'"

Murray groaned. "That just means they need more cash for their next re-election campaigns."

Ruth Ann smirked. "Your words, not mine."

He pointed at her notebook. "Yeah, well, make sure that's exactly how the people read it."

She tapped her notepad. "Oh, and a new factory's coming to town."

Murray's brow lifted. "What kind?"

"Textiles. They're promising fifty new jobs by next fall."

Murray exhaled through his nose. "Alright, we'll give it space, but I don't want that water rate hike getting buried beneath some 'good economic news' smoke screen. Keep it front and center."

"You got it, Chief."

As he walked away, the scent of roses still lingered behind him.

His last stop was Philip Goldstein, the paper's newest cub reporter. Fresh out of college, Philip still had that nervous energy, always straightening his tie and double-checking his notes even when he didn't need to.

Murray clapped a heavy hand on his shoulder, nearly knocking the poor kid into his typewriter.

"Goldstein! Good shots on the US-31 bypass construction."

Philip stammered, his mouth opening and closing like a fish gasping for air. "Uh—thank you, Chief! I—I just thought—"

Murray cut him off with a wave of his cigar. "Tell me. That framing on the overpass shot—that a calculated move, or was it dumb luck?"

Philip blinked, then swallowed hard. "Uh… a little bit of both?"

Murray grinned. "Good answer. You keep that honesty, kid. It'll serve you well."

Philip nodded furiously, clearly relieved he hadn't been chewed out.

Murray straightened up and took a slow look around the newsroom.

It was a living thing, this place. You could hear it in the clicking typewriters; the murmured phone calls, the occasional curse from a reporter trying to meet a deadline.

You could feel it in the ink-stained hands, the smudged notepads, the half-empty coffee cups that fueled the night crew.

He adjusted his cigar between his fingers, then raised his voice loud enough for everyone to hear.

"Alright, listen up! It's a busy damn day—fires, floods, politics, and progress. You know what that means?"

The room went quiet for half a beat. Then, from Esther's desk—

"It means we're getting paid?"

Laughter rippled through the newsroom.

Murray smirked. "Damn right. Now go earn it."

He turned on his heel and walked back toward his office, leaving a wave of renewed energy in his wake.

Dad leaned back in his chair, shaking his head with a smile. "I didn't understand it at the time, but later in my career, I realized why that man and that newspaper mattered so much. The *Traverse City Post* wasn't just a business. It was the backbone of the town. And Murray was the one making sure it kept standing."

Dad's voice carried that familiar weight again—the kind that only surfaced when he spoke about Murray Bernard.

"When it came to dollars and cents for education, the Chief was supportive," he said, a small but knowing smile tugging at the corner of his mouth.

I sat forward. "Supportive? How? Tuition reimbursement?"

Dad let out a dry chuckle. "If you asked him that, he'd probably laugh in your face. 'This ain't college, kid. You learn by doing.' But he made damn sure his employees had every opportunity to get better at their jobs."

"How?"

Dad tilted his head. "Workshops. Training sessions. If you worked in composition, camera, or printing press production, you didn't just show up and do the same thing every day. He sent people to learn from the best."

There was always something changing in the printing industry—new machines, better techniques, faster ways to set up layouts. And Murray made sure his employees stayed ahead of the game.

Dad tapped the side of his chair, his mind drifting to those days.

"If there was a new way to print cleaner, faster, or sharper—Murray didn't just read about it—He sent his guys to learn it firsthand."

I raised an eyebrow. "And everyone went?"

Dad snorted. "Oh, not always willingly. Some of the old-timers in press production weren't exactly thrilled about having to sit in a conference room listening to some industry expert talk about 'the future of offset printing.'"

He leaned back, shaking his head with a chuckle.

"But Murray didn't care. He'd drag them there if he had to. I remember one time, the lead press operator — Big Al McPherson — grumbled all week about having to go to a training in Chicago. He said he'd been working on presses since before the guy teaching the class was even born."

I smirked. "Did he end up going?"

Dad grinned. "Not only did he go — he came back raving about it. Wouldn't stop talking about 'this new ink-roller system' for weeks. That's the thing about Murray — he knew how to push people into being better, even when they fought him on it."

Dad's fingers trailed over an old newspaper clipping in his album, his eyes scanning the bold black-and-white headline:

BERNARD INTRODUCES OFFSET PRINTING TO POST

"You see this?" he said, tapping the page. "This was huge. We went from hot-metal linotypes to modern offset presses in record time."

I nodded. "That's a big change. Was there pushback?"

Dad exhaled, rubbing his temples. "Oh, plenty. You know how it is—people don't like change, especially when it threatens their way of doing things. But Murray? He didn't wait for people to get comfortable."

He flipped to another page, revealing a yellowed article from a few years later.

MANISTEE COUNTY WEEKLIES MERGE

Dad tapped the photo of Murray standing in front of the newly upgraded printing facility.

"He didn't just stop at the Post," he said. "Once he had offset printing running like a machine, he bought up a group of weeklies in Manistee County—and just like that, they weren't small papers anymore. They were part of something bigger."

I whistled. "He was building an empire."

Dad smirked. "And he was just getting started."

Dad turned the page again, this time landing on another clipping. The headline jumped out immediately:

BUCKEYE STATE NEWSPAPER ACQUIRED

I looked up. "That was his first move outside Michigan, right?"

Dad nodded. "Yep. First Ohio paper, Delphos Herald. And let me tell you, it wasn't in great shape when he got it."

I scanned the article. "It says here they were still using linotype machines."

"Exactly. Old as dirt. Type set by hand, one letter at a time, like it was still the 1920s. The place was struggling. Then Murray comes in, rips out the old machinery, installs offset printing, and modernizes the whole operation."

"And then?"

Dad chuckled. "Then he did what he always did — started buying up more county seat and community weeklies nearby."

Besides Mr. Bernard building them editorially into winning awards, "he had to keep those six-figure Goss printing presses making revenue. Which he did, two-three hundred thousand press runs, printing full color shoppers of major grocery chains, sandwiched between the deadlines of the weeklies and two dailies. Lights stayed on 24-7," recalled Dad.

The acquisitions no longer needed to be housed in those big old buildings since Delphos now became the central production site. "He sold them off, leased space for news-advertising and business operations in those modern designed strip malls. This exposure increased advertising revenue not only for the paper, but also they placed them in the nearby newspapers."

He closed the album, running his palm over the worn leather cover.

"That's what separated him, Benny. He didn't just buy papers—he made them better."

Dad leaned back, stretching his arms behind his head. His voice was quieter now, as if he was speaking more to himself than to me.

"Those were the days when nights and days seemed all the same."

He let out a small laugh, shaking his head.

"But I was given an opportunity to learn the business from the ground up. When I compare my college days with the Post, there's no contest."

I tilted my head. "Because of Murray?"

Dad's eyes flicked up, locking onto mine.

"Because real education doesn't come from a classroom. It comes from doing."

He tapped the side of the album. "I learned every part of this business—not just how to write, but how to layout pages, how to operate a press, how to deal with people."

He let out a small chuckle.

"And I got paid for it, too!"

I could hear the admiration in Dad's voice. Murray wasn't just a boss—he was a leader.

"Murray wasn't the kind of guy to sit in some high-rise office counting money."

I nodded. "He actually gave a damn."

Dad grinned. "Damn right, he did. He knew every single person who worked for him. The typesetters, the pressmen, the delivery drivers. And he didn't just shake their hands at some company dinner once a year. He talked to them. Asked about their families. If someone had a kid heading to college, Murray made sure they had opportunities to learn skills that would set them up for life."

I shook my head, impressed. "Most business owners don't think that way."

Dad smirked. "That's why most business owners aren't remembered."

He exhaled, glancing down at the old clippings again. "Murray didn't just run newspapers," he said quietly. "He built futures."

'Nordman Lake Haven'

LOVE AFFAIR: 1956-1959

"Too much of a good thing can be wonderful."
Mae West

♥

Dad met my mom, Sarah Cohan, when she was beginning her junior year at the University of Michigan in Ann Arbor in the fall of 1956. She had just turned 19, and he was a senior, finishing his degree in journalism.

From everything I gathered over the years, their first meeting wasn't grand or dramatic—just simple, yet life-changing. They met during a student government event, one of those early autumn campus gatherings when everyone returned and the leaves on the *Diag* were just beginning to shift to gold and red.

Still, Dad never missed a chance to embellish his version of the story.

As he always liked to say, with that slight grin of his, *"I knew she was the one."*

By then, I had learned all about my parents'

banter—what I called their 'head games'—the playful, back-and-forth jabs that always ended with laughter. And sure enough, as soon as Dad declared his undying certainty about Mom, she would slip into her best Mae West impression, her voice smooth but sharp enough to make her point, *"And don't you forget it, sweet thing."*

Dad never took that lying down. He would fire back with a grin, "I won't, Mrs. Grabowsky, because our association is similar to a pig's affinity for mud."

It was their signature way—a love rooted in teasing and sharp wit, but underlined with real devotion.

But while love was in the air for my parents, 1956 in Michigan was a year of both hardship and hope, and their story was unfolding right in the middle of it all.

September was a busy time for Michigan and the country. Political waves were swept through Detroit and other major cities as my mom and dad were starting their story.

Just as classes were resumed at the 'UMich' on Monday, September 6, 1956, U.S. Presidential candidate Adlai Stevenson marched in Detroit's Labor Day Parade, joined by a massive crowd of 75,000 people. The city streets were alive with banners, speeches, and calls for action, as Stevenson outlined his 'New America' plan, promising better education and health care for American citizens.

It wasn't just politics that shaped the year. Michigan had seen its share of tragedy earlier in 1956, and the echoes of those events were still fresh.

On April 2, 1956, a devastating tornado outbreak struck western Michigan, particularly Grand Rapids, causing catastrophic damage. Entire neighborhoods were torn apart. The tornado killed 18 people and injured hundreds more, leaving a lasting scar on the city and surrounding communities. Families were displaced, homes were flattened, and for many Michiganders, that spring storm was still a heavy memory by the time fall rolled around.

Just over a month later, on May 12, 1956, another round of violent tornadoes ripped through central and eastern Michigan, slamming into Detroit and Flint. Those storms claimed another nine lives, destroying homes and scattering businesses. For a state already on edge from natural disasters, 1956 was a year that tested its resilience.

Despite the destruction, 1956 was also a year of growth, invention, and pride for Michigan.

While my parents were flirting on campus and exchanging clever remarks, Detroit was still known as the 'Motor City' with Ford, General Motors, and Chrysler all in full production, fueling the country's booming car culture.

That same year, the Mackinac Bridge, one of the greatest engineering marvels in American history, was well underway in construction, finally linking Michigan's Upper and Lower Peninsulas. The bridge would eventually become a practical connection and a symbol of the state's unity and strength.

In sports, the Detroit Tigers gave fans a reason to hope. While they weren't in a championship season, baseball games at Briggs Stadium were still a favorite weekend pastime, and families gathered around radios to listen to games, just as much as they tuned in to the political speeches echoing from Detroit.

Also, Michigan's universities were growing fast. 'UMich' itself was already a hub of intellectual energy, progressive thinking, and political activism, creating a rich background for young minds like my mom and dad.

The Michigan State Normal College soon became Eastern Michigan University, and Wayne State University was expanding, giving more students access to higher education—part of that post-war push toward the American dream.

So while the streets of Grand Rapids were still being rebuilt, and Detroit's factories were busy stamping out Chevys and Fords, my mom and dad were laying their own foundation.

Sharp as ever, Mom was working toward her education degree, already thinking about the kind of classroom she wanted to lead. Dad, with his nose buried in newspapers and his eye on writing, was building the skills that would lead him to a lifetime of storytelling and editing.

They found each other during this era of rebuilding and dreaming, struggles and hopeful beginnings.

Looking back, I realize that their sharp words and teasing banter were just a reflection of a deeper love that carried them through not only good times but the hard ones, too.

They had witnessed the world around them change—from political upheavals to natural disasters and the unstoppable march of progress—and through it all, they built a bond as strong as any steel frame that came out of Detroit's factories.

Whenever Dad would tell me about the moment he first saw Mom on that autumn day in Ann Arbor, he always ended with the same smirk and the same words:

"I knew she was the one."

And Mom, never missing her cue, would chime in with a sly grin and that Mae West twang:

"And don't you forget it, sweet thing."

Though their love story began quietly, their days at the University of Michigan were anything but ordinary.

If anyone could picture them, it was like watching Katie and Hubbell in *"The Way We Were"*—two young people standing at opposite ends of every discussion but somehow always drawn together.

Dad was pounding the campus pavement, working as a reporter for the university newspaper, catching every political rally, football game, and campus dispute. His typewriter was practically an extension of his body.

Mom—Sarah Cohan—was no less determined. She threw herself into women's and children's advocacy groups, especially on the issue of women's access to spaces like the Michigan Union, which until recently had only admitted women with male escorts.

"I'm not going to wait at a door until some guy walks me in like I'm supposed to have a chaperone everywhere I go," she would say, hands firmly on her hips, staring down anyone who dared to challenge her.

Dad loved telling how he first noticed her—not because she was the loudest in the room, but because she never backed down, and she knew exactly what she stood for.

"She had a fire," he used to say, with a grin. "Sharp as a tack and not afraid to let anyone know it."

One of the first times Dad tried to talk to her, he showed up at a campus meeting where she was speaking about children's education rights. She was standing on a chair, addressing a crowd of students gathered on the Diag, her voice strong over the rustle of autumn leaves.

Dad sidled up next to a friend and whispered, "Who is she?"

His friend just laughed. "Sarah Cohan. Good luck, man. She'll tear you apart if you don't know what you're talking about."

Dad watched her for the rest of the speech, captivated.

Later that week, he approached her under the guise of writing a piece on women's access to the Michigan Union, though everyone knew it was just an excuse.

"I'm covering this for the paper," he said casually, flipping open his notebook. "Maybe you can give me a quote?"

She raised an eyebrow at him, smirking.

"A quote? Or are you hoping I'll do your thinking for you?" she shot back.

Dad chuckled, caught but not deterred. "Maybe a little of both," he admitted, and that was enough to break through her sharp edge.

They talked for over an hour that first time — about everything from campus politics to literature to how they both thought the university administration should do more to fix the disaster that was dormitory food service, especially after the near-riot that had broken out in the men's dorms over terrible meals.

"I mean, really," Sarah said, shaking her head. "It's hard to change the world on an empty stomach."

Dad laughed, scribbling something in his notebook, though he later admitted he wasn't writing anything—he just wanted an excuse to watch her talk.

Of course, it wasn't all activism and campus news.

Despite their sharp minds and strong beliefs, they were just a guy and a girl in college falling in love.

Saturdays in the fall were reserved for football games, and even though neither of them was a die-hard sports fan, they would bundle up in thick sweaters and walk together to Michigan Stadium, surrounded by crowds of students and alumni.

Dad loved to tell how, on October 6, 1956, they went to watch Michigan play Michigan State. 101,001 people packed into the stadium. It was supposed to be Michigan's game, especially after dominating the first half. But the turnovers had cost them, and Michigan State won 9 –0.

"I told you we should've left at halftime," Mom teased as they walked back to campus.

"And miss you throwing popcorn at the ref?" Dad grinned. "Not a chance."

When they weren't sparring in words or watching football, they escaped the noise of campus, heading out to the lakes around Ann Arbor—Frain's Lake, Murray's Lake, Whitmore Lake, and Four Mile Lake.

Dad would rent a rowboat, and they would spend lazy afternoons on the water, sometimes rowing, sometimes just drifting.

"You know you're rowing in circles, right?" Sarah laughed one afternoon as Dad struggled to keep the boat straight on Whitmore Lake.

"Circles are part of my strategy," Dad insisted, pretending to adjust his grip on the oars like a pro. "Keeps us from going too far away from shore. Safety first."

She splashed water at him, shaking her head, and he grinned like a fool, watching the sunlight dance off her hair.

Sometimes, they brought books—she would read to him, often works on philosophy, politics, or education reform, and he'd lean back, listening, occasionally throwing in a sarcastic comment to make her pause and laugh.

Other times, they'd stop at a small lakeside diner for ice cream—Sarah always getting vanilla, Dad swearing by chocolate malt, and then they'd argue about whose choice was better.

Despite all their differences—his world of newsprint and deadlines, her world of causes and classrooms—they found common ground in their dreams for the future.

Sitting under trees by the water, they talked about the kind of world they wanted to build together—a world where every child had access to education, where women didn't need an escort to walk into a building on their own campus, where voices that were too often silenced would finally be heard.

"I want to teach kids to think for themselves," Sarah said once, leaning her head on his shoulder as they watched the sunset over Four Mile Lake. "Not just memorize facts, but really think."

Dad reached over, taking her hand in his.

"And I want to write about people like you," he said softly. "People who aren't afraid to stand up for something real."

She smiled, turning her face toward him, eyes shining in the fading light.

"You'll probably write about me making you row in circles."

"Definitely," he said, laughing. "But I'll make you look good."

You could tell Mom and Dad were not the usual married couple who grew accustomed to one another over the years. There was no going through the motions, no distant smiles over dinner.

They showered each other with never-ending best friend support, often standing as each other's biggest champions, loudest critics, and constant audience for all things big and small.

Even as a child, I noticed how they would drift off into their own world, even in a room full of people. They had an endless stream of this or that debates, as though they never tired of learning each other's opinions, even if the topics were as trivial as which brand of coffee was better.

"I'm telling you, Sarah, nothing beats Maxwell House."

Mom would laugh that light, knowing laugh of hers. "Maxwell House tastes like mud, Nathan. If you want a real cup of coffee, you drink Chock Full o'Nuts."

Dad would throw his hands up, grinning. "Says

the woman who still puts two sugars in her coffee and calls it strong!"

She'd lean in closer with that twinkle in her eye, "Well, some of us aren't bitter enough to take it black like death."

Then he'd lean in, too, dropping his voice in mock seriousness. "Death wishes it could brew a cup as strong as mine."

That was them. Constantly sparring but always smiling.

And it didn't stop at coffee. They debated movies, music, books, politics, and even which side of the bed was better.

"The left side's mine, Sarah, you know that."

"Well, tonight you're getting the right side, Nathan. You've been stealing my pillow all week."

"I steal pillows because I need something to hold onto when you roll away like a bandit."

She would laugh, shaking her head, but her hand would always find his under the covers.

As I grew older, I realized that the love they shared wasn't just friendship—it was a fire that burned quietly but powerfully.

Of course, as a kid, the squeaky bed was just a noise I chalked up to restless nights.

But by the time I was older, I understood.

It wasn't just tossing and turning that made the springs groan in protest.

It was two people savoring the fruits of a love not dimmed by time, lovers entwined in the deepest kind of knowing that comes from years of trust and passion.

It was the kind of connection that wasn't embarrassed by age or responsibility.

They loved like newlyweds but with the ease of old souls.

The soft murmurs I sometimes overheard through the thin walls weren't fights or complaints, but words of affection, teasing, and shared laughter.

Sometimes, I would hear Dad whisper something late at night, and Mom's soft chuckle would follow.

Once, when I was about fifteen, walking past their room to get a glass of water, I overheard Dad say, "Sarah, if you keep looking at me like that, I'm going to think you want something."

To which she replied, voice warm and amused, "What if I do?"

Even then, I couldn't help but smile. They were still deeply in love—body, heart, and soul.

And they carried that connection into their everyday life.

Their chit-chat was constant, natural, and could fill the air like a favorite song on repeat.

Mom would read her book at breakfast while Dad skimmed the newspaper, and without even looking up, one would start.

"Do you think it's better to live by the water or in the city?" Mom would ask casually.

Dad, without pausing, would reply, "Water. You can fish. You can swim. And nobody bothers you."

"But in the city, you can walk to the market and hear people's stories."

"And hear their complaints," Dad muttered, folding the paper. "Give me the sound of waves over car horns any day."

"But where would you get your coffee, Nathan?"

He'd glance at her with a smirk. "I'd fish for it."

She'd grin right back. "Fish don't give coffee, sweetheart."

"Well," he'd say, leaning back, "then I guess I'll have to learn to live off love."

Mom would shake her head, but I'd see that secret smile she only gave him.

Even when discussing more serious things, they knew how to keep it light, always looping back to each other.

Once, when talking about Dad's dream to write a book and Mom's plans to start a children's art program, she said, "You write the book, Nathan, and I'll make sure the kids have something to read when they're done drawing."

"Deal," he said. "And when you're famous for teaching little Picassos, I'll write their story."

"You'll make me sound taller, right?" she teased.

"Always," he replied.

Diploma put to Test

Upon Dad's graduation in 1957, true to his passion and calling, he accepted a reporter's post with the Traverse City Post, covering the county beat.

He had always wanted to write, but now, it wasn't just campus news or student debates—it was real life, and real people, with stories that mattered far beyond the university halls.

In a town where every face was familiar, and every event carried the weight of community, Dad quickly became known for telling the stories that others were too timid or too hardened to write. His writing wasn't flowery or dramatic. It was clear, sharp, and human—and people responded to that.

Within months, he built a loyal following of readers looking for his byline because they knew his stories would tug at their hearts but would not flinch from the hard truths.

Among the earliest stories that showed Dad's deep sensitivity to the human element was his coverage of the Carrick family tragedy—a story that shook the entire state of Michigan.

On October 30, 1957, eight members of the Carrick family—from the tiny Upper Peninsula community of Pickford, Michigan—perished in a house fire that swept through their home in the middle of the night.

Dad traveled north to Pickford, and as he would later recount, it was one of the hardest assignments of his early career.

He spoke quietly with neighbors, the fire chief, and even the sole surviving family member, who was left to pick up the pieces of a life reduced to ash.

Dad's story did not shy away from the horror of

what had happened, but more than that, he focused on the lives that had been lost, writing about the Carrick children — their hopes, their daily routines, and the simple joys of life on the Upper Peninsula. He brought to light the human loss behind the headline, and readers across Michigan felt the depth of the tragedy as if it had happened next door.

I remember Mom saying later, "That story tore your father up. He carried those kids in his heart for a long time after."

But Dad's journalism wasn't limited to covering loss — he also reported on the darker sides of society, where justice had to be pursued, even when it was uncomfortable.

One of the most high-profile stories Dad covered was the murder trial of Herman Barmore — a case that gripped the entire state and made national headlines.

In Muskegon, Barmore, an ex-convict, stood accused of the brutal murder of 12-year-old Boy Scout, Peter Gorham, a boy who had been shot and left in the wilderness near Camp Wabaningo while returning from a hike in July 1955.

By the time the trial concluded in 1957, it had become the longest trial in Muskegon County history.

Dad was there for every day of that courtroom saga.

He sat quietly in the back, notebook in hand,

watching the boy's grieving family, taking in every word of testimony, and following the tense, methodical work of both the prosecution and defense.

Unlike some reporters who focused only on the courtroom drama, Dad made sure to give readers the full weight of what had happened to Peter—a young boy with dreams of becoming a wildlife biologist, a boy who loved the outdoors, whose life was cut short by a senseless act of violence.

He also wrote about the reactions of the Muskegon community—how neighbors supported the Gorham family, how people lined the courthouse steps each day, and how parents of other Boy Scouts watched the trial, wondering how to explain to their children what had happened to Peter.

Dad's reports were painfully honest, but never cruel. He understood the responsibility he carried in shaping how the community would remember Peter Gorham—not just as a victim, but as a boy with a story of his own.

Mom once told me, "Your father took no pleasure in writing about death, but he believed the truth had to be told. And he never let anyone forget that Peter was more than a headline—he was a son, a friend, and a boy with a future."

Even in those early years, what set Dad apart was that he didn't just report the news—he lived it, felt it, and made sure others did too.

He always said, "If a story doesn't move you, you have no business writing it."

It wasn't long before the community recognized his name not just as a byline in the 𝕿𝖗𝖆𝖛𝖊𝖗𝖘𝖊 𝕮𝖎𝖙𝖞 𝕻𝖔𝖘𝖙, but as a voice for those who couldn't speak for themselves—families grieving, communities healing, victims needing justice.

He balanced the hard stories with pieces that warmed people's hearts, too—stories about local farmers, small-town celebrations, and heroic acts by ordinary people. But he never let the community turn away from the dark moments either.

And through it all, Mom was his anchor.

She would often sit at the kitchen table, reading over his articles before he submitted them.

"I don't want to make this family's pain worse, Sarah," he'd say, rubbing his eyes.

She would hold his hand and say, "Then write it like you're speaking to them. Like they're reading every word you put down."

Dad always said those first years together were his "romance period."

"I had a light heart back then," he would tell me, almost wistfully. "I was humbled by your mother's love for me. It gave me direction. It made me want to write only the truth."

He never shied away from talking about how Mom's love grounded him and kept him honest, both on the page and in life.

They married a year after she received her degree in education in 1958—a time when they were both young, hopeful, and eager to start their life together.

Mom would always laugh as she recalled how it all came together.

"Luckily, I sent out my resume to Traverse City Schools, and I was hired almost immediately," she'd say, her voice still filled with wonder at how smoothly things had worked out. "I can only surmise—it was fate."

Dad, never missing a beat, would chime in with a smirk:

"Yes, and your mother learned real quick in her first year of teaching that children are fickle creatures. One day, they love you, and the next, they're ready to attach a pipe bomb to the chassis of your car!"

Mom would roll her eyes at his exaggeration, but her smile said she knew there was some truth in the humor.

On May 23, 1959, they were married at Congregation Beth Shalom, Michigan's oldest synagogue in continuous use, built in 1885 right in the heart of Traverse City.

Mom would often describe the synagogue's warm wooden interior, the old stained-glass windows filtering the sunlight, and the way it felt to stand before their family and friends surrounded by history and faith.

It was a traditional Jewish wedding, rich with custom and meaning.

I can still hear her voice when she spoke about walking around Dad seven times, her dress trailing behind her.

"I remember circling him, and I felt like I was binding us together with every step. Each turn was like a promise I was making. Seven circles, for seven days of creation, and to create our new life together."

Dad would nod adding, "And I was standing there trying not to look nervous."

Of course, when the moment came to break the glass, Dad always liked to joke:

"They said it's supposed to remind us that even in joy, we remember sorrow. But I think your mother just liked watching me stomp on things!"

After the ceremony, they had a traditional reception, filled with joy and celebration.

There was a feast of chicken and fish dishes, the tables lined with plates of roasted vegetables, kugel, and warm challah bread.

And when the band struck up "Hava Nagila," Dad and Mom were hoisted onto chairs, surrounded by family and friends dancing the Hora, clapping, and singing.

Mom would laugh when she told me about it, remembering the look of terror on Dad's face as he tried to stay balanced in the chair.

"He thought he was going to fall right into the gefilte fish!" she would say, laughing so hard she'd wipe tears from her eyes.

But Dad always grinned, "I didn't fall—because she had my hand the whole time."

After all the dancing and celebration, they traveled to Green Lake, Wisconsin, where they spent their honeymoon at the *Manor on the Lake*—a historic lakeside retreat that would become their summer sanctuary for years to come.

Mom's face would soften as she remembered those first days together.

"We didn't have much. But sitting by that lake, watching the sun go down, it felt like we had everything."

For the next six years, they returned to the *Manor on Green Lake* every summer, sometimes just the two of them, and later, when I was born, with me in tow.

It became their special place, a quiet refuge away from the world where they could reconnect and dream.

And every year, without fail, Dad would stand on the porch of that little lakeside cabin, staring out across the water, and say,

"Someday, Sarah, if this place ever goes on the market, I'm going to buy it."

Mom would laugh, knowing it was both a dream and a vow.

"I'm holding you to that, Nathan," she'd tease.

He would grin. "You always do."

And like so much in their life, Dad's quiet persistence paid off.

In 1974, when I was nearly 14, his dream came true.

Continued on Page 177

"Destiny"

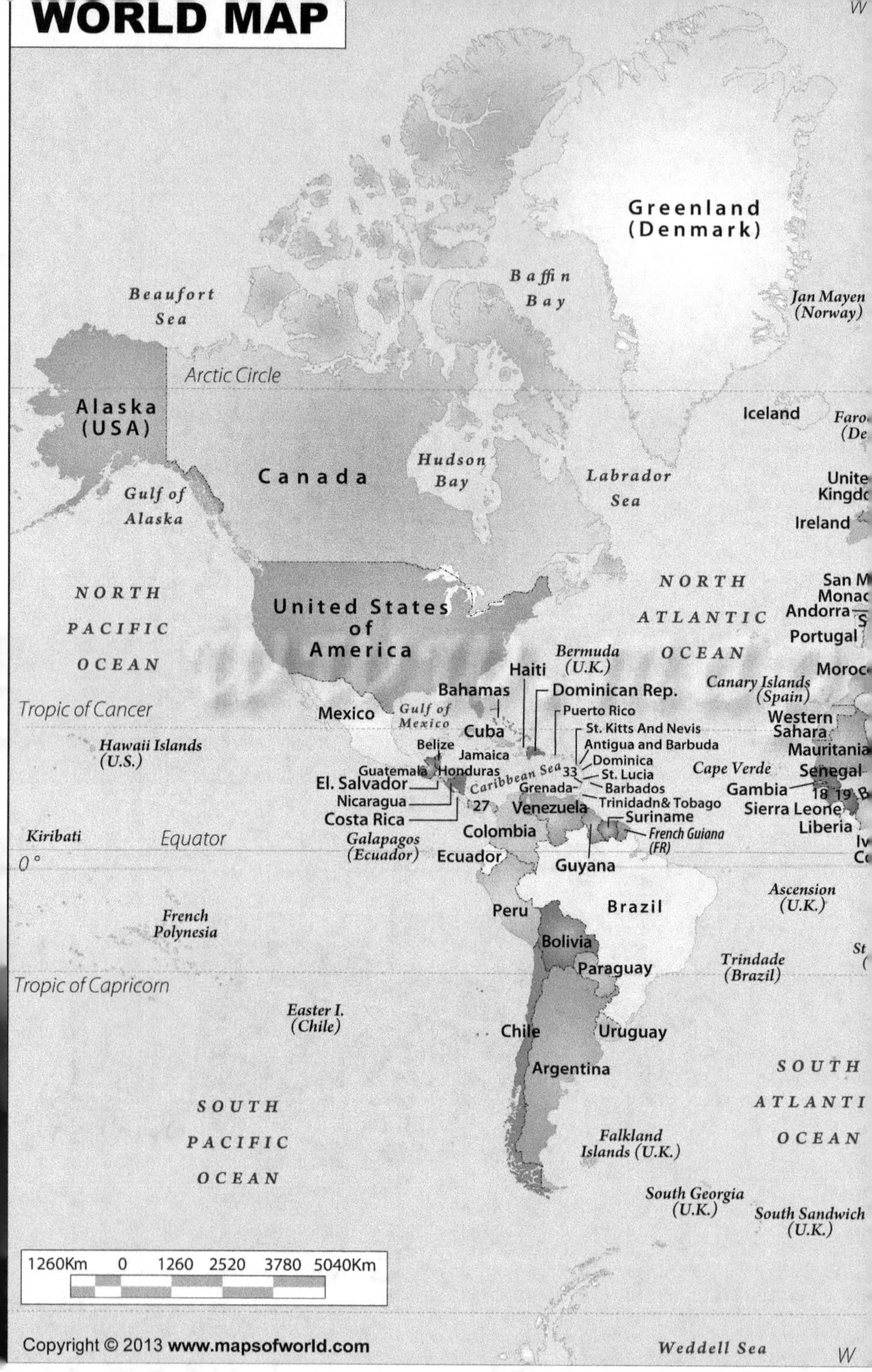

WORLD MAP
Greenland (Denmark)
Jan Mayen (Norway)
Beaufort Sea
Baffin Bay
Arctic Circle
Iceland
Faro (De
Alaska (USA)
Canada
Hudson Bay
Labrador Sea
Unite Kingdo
Ireland
Gulf of Alaska
NORTH PACIFIC OCEAN
NORTH ATLANTIC OCEAN
San M
Monac
Andorra
Portugal
United States of America
Tropic of Cancer
Bermuda (U.K.)
Moroc
Canary Islands (Spain)
Western Sahara
Mauritania
Hawaii Islands (U.S.)
Mexico
Gulf of Mexico
Haiti
Bahamas
Dominican Rep.
Cuba
Puerto Rico
St. Kitts And Nevis
Antigua and Barbuda
Belize
Jamaica
Dominica
Cape Verde
Senegal
Guatemala
Honduras
Caribbean Sea
33
St. Lucia
El. Salvador
Grenada
Barbados
Gambia
18 19 B
Nicaragua
27
Trinidadn& Tobago
Sierra Leone
Costa Rica
Venezuela
Suriname
Liberia
Galapagos (Ecuador)
Colombia
French Guiana (FR)
Iv
Kiribati
Equator
0°
Ecuador
Guyana
Co
Peru
Brazil
Ascension (U.K.)
French Polynesia
Bolivia
Paraguay
Trindade (Brazil)
St
Tropic of Capricorn
Easter I. (Chile)
Chile
Uruguay
Argentina
SOUTH ATLANTI OCEAN
SOUTH PACIFIC OCEAN
Falkland Islands (U.K.)
South Georgia (U.K.)
South Sandwich (U.K.)
1260Km   0   1260 2520 3780 5040Km
Copyright © 2013 www.mapsofworld.com
Weddell Sea

N

ARCTIC OCEAN

Zemlya Frantsa-Iosifa
Oktyabr'skoy Revolyutsil
Kotelny Island
Laptev Sea
East Siberian Sea
Wrangel Island
Novaya Zemlya
Kara Sea
Barents Sea
Finland
Arctic Circle
Bering Sea
Russia
Estonia
Latvia
Lithuania
Belarus
Ukraine
13
Romania
31
Bulgaria
Black Sea
Caspian Sea
Aral Sea
Kazakhstan
Mongolia
Sea of Okhotsk
North Korea
Sea of Japan (East Sea)
Greece
Turkey
Georgia
Azerbaijan
Uzbekistan
Kyrgyzstan
China
South Korea
Japan
PACIFIC OCEAN
n Sea
16
17
Syria
Armenia
Turkmenistan
Tajikistan
32
Iraq
Iran
Afghanistan
Bhutan
East China Sea
Jordan
Kuwait
Nepal
Myanmar (Burma)
Taiwan
Israel
Bahrain
Qatar
Pakistan
India
Egypt
Saudi Arabia
U.A.E.
Bangladesh
Laos
Philippine Sea
Northern Mariana Islands
Red Sea
Oman
Arabian Sea
Bay of Bengal
Thailand
26
Vietnam
Guam
Marshall Islands
Sudan
Eritrea
Yemen
Philippines
Palau
Federated States of Micronesia
South Sudan
Ethiopia
Somalia
Djibouti
Maldives
Sri Lanka
Sumatra
Malaysia
Brunei
Kiribati
0°
Uganda
25
Kenya
Andaman Is.
Indonesia
Papua New Guinea
Nauru
Tuvalu
m. Rep. ongo
Burundi
Singapore
Java
East Timor
Soloman Islands
Walis & Fatuna
Tanzania
Seychelles
Comoros
Mayotte
Cocos Is. (Aus.)
Christmas Is. (Aus.)
Coral Sea
Vanuatu
Samoa
Fiji
Zambia 28
Madagascar
Mauritius
Reunion
INDIAN OCEAN
New Caledonia (France)
Tonga
Zimbabwe
tswana
Mozambique
Swaziland
Lesotho
outh frica
Australia
Great Australian Bight
Tasman Sea
New Zealand
North Island
Tasmania
South Island

rlands
m
nbourg
erland
nia
a
a and
govina
Republic
kia

10. Austria
11. Hungary
12. Serbia
13. Moldova
14. Macedonia
15. Albania
16. Cyprus
17. Lebanon
18. Guinea-Bissau
19. Guinea

20. Ghana
21. Togo
22. Benin
23. Cameroon
24. Equatorial Guinea
25. Rwanda
26. Cambodia
27. Panama
28. Malawi

29. Liechtenstein
30. Montenegro
31. Kosovo
32. Palestinian Territories
33. St. Vincent and the Grenadines

SOUTHERN OCEAN
Antarctic Circle
NTARCTICA

"Destinations"

with the help of a local realtor, a former B&B came on the market, and Dad had no time to follow his quest and vow to Mom.

I still remember the day they told me—we were sitting at the kitchen table, the newspaper spread out in front of Dad, and Mom holding a cup of coffee between her hands.

"Well, Benjamin," Dad said, glancing at me over the rim of his glasses, "looks like we're going to have a home on the lake."

Mom was beaming, and I could tell this wasn't just about buying a property—it was about fulfilling a promise made on a porch years before.

A dream built with love, laughter, and quiet hope.

From that day on, their honeymoon retreat became our family home, where life slowed down, and every sunset was a reminder of the life they had built together—a life rooted in love, held together by dreams, and carried forward by promises kept.

"Tall Timbers"

CAREER OFFER 1966

"If you work just for money, you'll never make it, but if you love what You're doing and you always put the customer first, success will be yours."

Ray Croc

T he fall of 1966 was a double celebration in our
house.

My grandparents aka Nana and Asa were
celebrating their 30th wedding anniversary, and Dad was
officially named Editor of the 𝕿raverse 𝕮ity 𝕻ost. These
were the milestones that made them reflective but also
proud of how far they had come.

Also, for Dad, the recognizing hard work began a
new chapter in his journalism career, a symbol of arrival.
But while this moment lifted his spirit, it was quickly
overshadowed by the weight of Michigan's troubled
headlines.

1966 was no ordinary year.

It was a year when Michigan's urban and natural
landscapes were clouded with tragedy and unrest.

Dad, now Editor, was right at the heart of it, trying to keep the community informed and united in a time of uncertainty.

One of the hardest stories to write came in late November, when news broke that the ore carrier SS Daniel J. Morrell had sunk in the icy waters of Lake Huron.

The ship had 29 crew members aboard, and only one survived. The lake that had been Michigan's lifeblood became its graveyard that night.

Dad followed the story relentlessly, often staying late into the night at the newspaper office, piecing together statements from the Coast Guard, grieving families, and survivors' accounts.

He never reported those details coldly. He wrote about the faces behind the names, about the men who went to work on the Morrell and never returned home—sons, brothers, fathers—whose empty chairs at the dinner table would be felt for generations.

Mom said she found him sitting quietly at the kitchen table one night, long after we had all gone to bed, staring at his notes with a cup of cold coffee beside him.

"It's not just a shipwreck, Sarah," he had said to her, rubbing his eyes. "It's an entire town's heartbreak."

But Michigan's waters weren't the only places where storms were brewing.

On August 30, violence erupted in Benton Harbor, where racial tensions and economic frustrations exploded into street riots.

When Governor George Romney ordered 1,790 National Guardsmen to the streets to restore order, it made

headlines nationwide—and once again, Dad was there to make sense of the chaos for the readers of the Post.

He knew it wasn't enough to report on broken windows and burned-out cars. Dad wanted people to understand what was underneath it all—the anger, the poverty, the inequality that had built up for too long.

Still, those stories wore on him.

"It's hard to write about people fighting when you know it's because nobody listened for too long," he would say.

If that wasn't enough, teachers' strikes shook the state in both the spring and fall of 1966, including walkouts in nearby counties.

For Mom, a teacher herself, these stories hit close to home.

She would sit across from Dad at the kitchen table, grading papers while he typed out editorials, both of them caught up in the same battle—just from different sides of the fight.

"I don't know how to write about this one, Sarah," Dad confessed one evening as she packed up her books after another long day. "I know too many of the teachers

walking those picket lines. They're good people. But the schools are struggling to stay open."

Mom looked at him thoughtfully.

"Then write it like that," she said simply. "Write it so people know it's not about sides. It's about fixing what's broken."

Through all of this, Mom was Dad's anchor—the steady hand that kept him from going under when the stories got too heavy to carry alone.

She knew what it took to keep Dad balanced, to remind him to step away from the paper and come back to real life, even if just for an evening.

"All work and no play makes Jack a dull boy," she would tease when he came home late, tossing his jacket over a chair and rubbing his temples.

"Yeah, well, Jack also has deadlines," he would reply with a wry smile, but then he'd let her pull him out to the porch for a breath of night air or agree to a quiet evening drive out to the lake, where the water calmed his mind the way nothing else could.

Mom knew—better than anyone—that Dad needed to see more than just the darkness he wrote about.

A Seedling meet by Chance

While my parents were spending a quiet weekend at their cabin in Suttons Bay, the kind of peaceful retreat they cherished, fate had other plans.

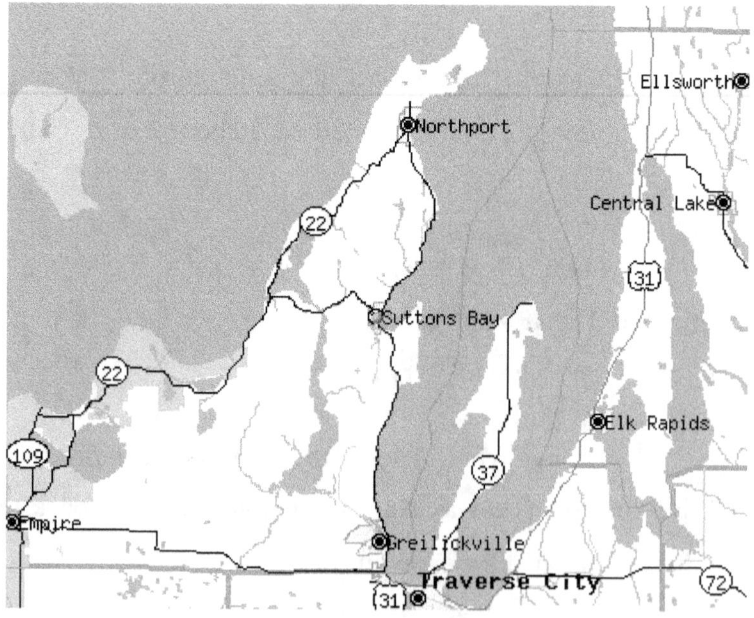

There, Dad met George Kuser, the head of the *Reuters News Agency*, at a local coffee shop that overlooked the bay's soft blue waters. Suttons Bay had been Kuser's boyhood home before his family relocated to Detroit, and he had come back for a visit, drawn to the place that still held childhood memories.

Dad was standing in line for coffee when Kuser approached, recognizing him instantly.

"You're Nathan Grabowsky, right?" Kuser asked, extending his hand with a knowing smile.

Dad looked up, a bit surprised but pleased, and shook his hand firmly.

"Guilty as charged," Dad said, grinning.

"I thought so. I've been a subscriber to the *Post* for years. Your stories about people here—there's something about them. You don't just tell the news; you get them to open up. I can tell you've got a natural way with people."

Dad laughed, "Sometimes, if you listen long enough, people tell you everything."

They found a quiet corner by the window, and what started as casual chit-chat over coffee soon became an animated conversation.

"You ever think about working for a bigger outfit?"

Kuser asked, taking a sip of his coffee.

Dad leaned back in his chair. "Sure, I think about it. But I've got a good thing going with the *Post*. They let me write what I care about."

Kuser nodded, "I respect that. But there's a whole world out there, Nathan. And we need good people — writers who see beyond the politics and get to the heart of the story."

They talked about everything from reporting and writing to world politics, including the growing tensions in the Middle East.

"Things are about to get worse over there," Kuser said, his tone serious. "Jerusalem's going to be the center of it all soon."

Dad, listened thoughtfully, knowing Kuser wasn't one to speak lightly about world affairs.

As they wrapped up their conversation, Kuser leaned forward and said,

"Listen, if you ever want to step into international work, I've got an opening coming up in our Detroit Bureau. It's foreign correspondence, but... you'd be based in Jerusalem."

Dad blinked, taken aback.

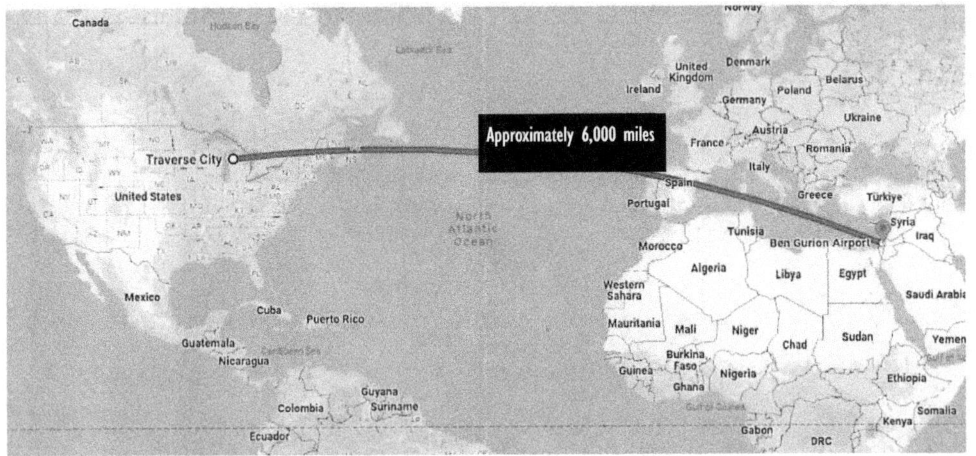

Suttons Bay is located in Leelanau County, Michigan and is a smaller inlet of Grand Traverse Bay, a bay of Lake Michigan. It is also within approximately 17 miles to Traverse City, county seat of Grand Traverse County, which also partly extends into Leelanau County.

Jerusalem is one of the oldest cities in the world, a city in the Southern Levant, on a plateau in the Judaean Mountains between the Mediterranean and the Dead Sea, and is considered holy to the three major Abrahamic religions of Judaism, Christianity and Islam.

"Jerusalem? That's a long way from Suttons Bay, George."

Kuser smiled, "Yeah, but a man like you would fit right in. You'd be covering history as it happens."

For Dad, the offer was as exciting as it was overwhelming. "You could say I was in a state of mental turmoil," he later told me. "My career with the *Post* was going somewhere, and your mother was finally building something of her own with her art program. And you — you were just about to start second grade."

Still, the idea took root.

Sensing Dad's hesitation, Kuster leaned back and said, "Think it over. No rush. But next year, that position will still be open."

Dad smiled, knowing he wasn't ready to say yes—but—he couldn't quite say no.

They left it at that, and soon, both men went back to enjoying the rest of the weekend—fishing on the bay, trading stories, and laughing like old friends.

By late spring of 1967, life had returned to its usual pace.

Dad was back to the *Post*, writing and editing. But one day, the phone rang as he sat in his office,

It was Kuser.

"Nathan, I'm calling to see if you've been following the news out of Israel."

Dad, of course, had. The Middle East was teetering on the edge of war.

"Hard not to follow it, George. Feels like the whole region's a match ready to be struck."

Kuser didn't waste time.

"We need you. War is coming, and we need someone who can tell the real story — someone people trust. Think about it."

Dad leaned back in his chair, running a hand over his face.

"It's a lot to ask, George. You know what's going on here. Sarah's program is taking off. Benjamin's still young. And I'm not sure I'm ready to pick up and move to Jerusalem."

Kuser's voice softened.

"I get it. But I wouldn't ask if I didn't think you could handle it. You have a way of cutting through the noise, Nathan. And believe me, Jerusalem's going to be nothing but noise."

Even as Dad mulled over the offer, he covered the local reactions to the brewing conflict, including the

Reuters News Agency   JUNE 6, 1967

Terror Looms On 'Hanukaland'?

By Nathan Grabowsky
Reuters Foregin International Editor

TEL AVIV — Israel and the Arab states went to war at dawn yesterday for the third time in two decades, and by nightfall both sides were claiming significant military victories.

Israel last night appeared headed toward a major military victory over her Arab enemies by smashing deeply into Egypt their way to the gates of the Jordan-held old city of Jersualem.

There were violent Arab counter reactions: breaks in diplomatic relations, interruptions to oil supplies, closing of the Suez Canal, though it was not blocked, and accusations that the United States and Britain had sent aircraft into combat on the Israeli side. This latter charge was angrily and categorically denied in Washington and London.

US President Johnson and Soviet Premier Kosygin have exchanged messages declaring a mutual desire to avoid an American-Soviet collision in the Middle East.

On the morning of June 5, 1967, the phone rang in a small apartment in Herzliya, an upmarket suburb a few miles north of Tel Aviv.

"Good morning, madam. This is Yuri speaking. Is your husband at home?" said a man's voice in English with a heavy Russian accent, sounding tense.

"I wish he were, Yuri," the woman answered. "He's been called up to the reserves."

"If he calls, tell him I need to meet with him urgently," the man on the line said before hanging up.

The caller was Yuri Kotov, an up-and-coming K.G.B. case officer.

Two and a half years earlier, he had recruited a man whose K.G.B. code name was Boy, a prominent young member of Israel's ruling Labor Party.

Since then, Boy had given Kotov a wealth of information on the party, and from his reserves post in military intelligence.

divided opinions within Michigan's communities.

He wrote a powerful piece capturing the rising tensions in Israel and the Arab world, and how those conflicts reverberated even in small towns like Traverse City.

His article drew a huge response, especially among readers sympathetic to Muwaffiq al-Allah, Syria's chief negotiator, who advocated for the Golan Heights recovery.

Dad captured both sides: Israel's desperate need for security and recognition, and the Arab world's demand for lost territory and justice for Palestinians.

It was balanced, but unflinching—a hallmark of his writing.

When Kuser read the article, he immediately called Dad back.

"Nathan, would it be possible to grant Reuters permission to reprint *'Terror Looms On 'Hanukaland'?"* Kuser asked, his voice full of conviction. "I want to run the story as the lead holiday feature throughout our entire print media network."

Dad told me later that he had sat there for a long time before answering.

He knew what that meant—exposure to a

worldwide audience, and stepping fully into the world of international journalism.

And when he finally answered Kuser, it was simple and clear:

"Yes. Run it!"

That moment — sitting at his desk, listening to Kuser on the other end of the line — was a turning point for Dad.

It wasn't just about taking the job.

It was about recognizing that his voice weighted Northern Michigan; that the stories he was meant to tell were bigger than anything he had written before.

And as he later told Mom that night, sitting at the kitchen table,

"I don't know where this is going to lead, Sarah. But I know I have to follow it."

She looked at him, quiet for a moment, before finally saying,

"Then we'll follow it together."

"Albert Einstein" 03-14-1879-04-18-1955

FOREIGN CONNECTION 1967-1973

"All life is an experiment. The more experiments you make the better."
Ralph Waldo Emerson

♥

K user leaned back in his chair. "The way you handled the Six-Day War coverage—brutal, honest. You captured what most reporters couldn't."

Dad's face grew serious. "Because I saw what others didn't want to see. I was standing on a rooftop in Jerusalem, and hearing the gunfire, watching tanks roll in. It wasn't some far-off battle—it was right there. People didn't understand how quickly everything changed. One minute, Israel was facing  annihilation, and the next, they controlled Jerusalem, the West Bank, Gaza, Sinai, and the Golan Heights. And behind it all, you could feel it—this wasn't over. It never really is."

Kuser took a long sip of his drink. "And now, it's all tangled up with what's going on in Vietnam. I mean, look at it—two different parts of the world, but both boiling over."

Dad nodded, running a hand through his hair. "Vietnam's a mess. America thought it could walk in, fight a quick war, and walk out victorious. But that jungle eats men alive. I talk to guys coming back—soldiers, photographers—every one of them haunted. And you can bet the Middle East is watching. They see how the U.S. bleeds over there, and they know exactly what that means for American influence here."

Kuser raised an eyebrow. "You think it's weakening America's hand in the Middle East?"

Dad took a long drag from his cigarette, his eyes fixed on the file of clippings stacked on the desk. The orange glow of the burning tip lit up the sharp lines of his face as the smoke curled into the air. Kuser sat across from him, leaning forward, elbows on knees, and a glass of scotch in hand.

"You've been in the middle of it all, haven't you?" Kuser asked, breaking the silence. "Your name is running on every major outlet. I just read your latest piece on Cairo—hard stuff."

Dad gave a slow nod, exhaling a thick cloud of smoke.

The room was heavy with smoke as Dad leaned back in his chair, swirling his glass absently. Kuser sat across from him, elbows on the table, listening carefully.

"You know," Dad said, exhaling a long breath, "when I covered the Six-Day War, I thought maybe that was it—maybe they'd fought it out and settled the score. But now?" He shook his head. "Now it feels like that was just the opening act."

Kuser raised an eyebrow. "What makes you say that? You think they're gearing up again?"

Dad looked out the window, watching the streetlights flicker in the distance. "You should see what I've seen in Cairo and Damascus. Troop movements, new Soviet tanks rolling in, and the way people talk in cafes—like something's coming. They're not over '67. Not by a long shot."

Kuser leaned in. "You think Sadat and Assad would risk another war? After what happened last time?"

Dad gave a dry laugh. "I think they have to. You don't lose half your country and just sit on your hands. And Sadat—he's not Nasser. He doesn't want to look weak. He's been publicly saying he'll do 'whatever it takes' to get Sinai back. Some people say he's bluffing. But I've been hearing from folks in the street, soldiers off duty—there's a real anger building."

"And Syria?" Kuser asked.

"They're still smarting over Golan. Assad's been tightening alliances, even making noise about joint action with Egypt. Some of it's probably posturing. But when I was in Damascus last, you could feel it—soldiers drilling in desert camps, Soviet advisors everywhere. Looks to me like they're preparing for something."

Kuser took a sip of his drink, thoughtful. "And the Palestinians?"

Dad nodded. "Yeah. Arafat's PLO is stronger than ever. After '67, they got kicked around, but now? They're running camps in Lebanon, Jordan, and even in the territories. Fatah is getting fighters trained and armed—again, a lot of Soviet weapons. And honestly, the longer Israel holds those lands, the more recruits the PLO gets."

He paused for a moment, leaning forward.

"And you know what's making it worse?" Dad continued. "America is so tied up in Vietnam, it's like people forgot about the Middle East. That whole mess is draining U.S. attention and money. Do you think Arafat doesn't know that? The Palestinians know the timing's better now than it's been in years."

Kuser nodded slowly. "Yeah, Vietnam's bleeding them dry. People back home are more focused on what's happening in Saigon than Jerusalem."

Dad flicked ash into a tray. "Exactly. And let me tell you—people think Israel is invincible after '67, but you talk to Israeli soldiers? They're nervous. They see the buildup in Egypt and Syria. They know if those two act together, Israel will be fighting on two fronts."

Kuser looked skeptical. "But do you think Egypt and Syria can really pull that off? I mean, can they coordinate well enough for a real attack?"

Dad shrugged. "I don't know. Maybe not. But if they do, it could be ugly. They've been getting serious hardware from the Soviets. SAM missiles, tanks, artillery. Israel's good, but they're stretched thin holding all that new land. And Yom Kippur is coming up soon."

Kuser looked at him sharply. "You think they'd attack on Yom Kippur?"

"I've heard whispers," Dad admitted. "Nothing solid. But think about it—Israel's most sacred day, a lot of soldiers at home, in synagogues. If you wanted to catch them off guard, that's when you do it."

Kuser leaned back, exhaling. "God, that'd be something."

"And if a war breaks out," Dad continued, "it won't stay regional. America will back Israel, like always. And you can bet the Soviets will back Egypt and Syria. It's a dangerous game."

"And oil?" Kuser asked, lowering his voice.

Dad tapped the ashtray. "I don't know. But I'll tell you this—if there's a war and America sides with Israel, the oil-producing Arab states might not take that quietly. I've heard talk in Kuwait, and Saudi—people are angry about American weapons going to Israel. There's been grumbling about using oil as leverage."

"But you think they'd really cut oil to the West?"

Dad shrugged. "I don't know. But if the fighting gets bad enough, and if America goes all in on Israel—maybe. They've got the power. And if they use it? Let's just say I wouldn't want to be a driver in New York or London if that happens."

Kuser ran a hand over his face, looking tired. "You've got to write this, Nathan. People need to know what's brewing over there."

Dad looked at him, jaw set. "I'm already working on it."

Kuser met his gaze. "Good. Because if you're right—and I think you might be—people are walking blindly into a storm."

Kuser swirled the ice in his glass. "You gonna write it?"

Dad leaned forward, resting his elbows on the table. His eyes, sharp and clear, locked with Kuser's. "Hell yes, I'm gonna write it. People need to know what's coming. They need to understand these aren't just wars in far-off deserts—these are battles that'll reach into every kitchen, every gas station back home."

There was a moment of silence between them, both men lost in their thoughts, hearing only the distant sounds of sirens and city life beyond the window.

Dad leaned back in his chair, and the room fell into silence for a moment., both men sitting with the weight of everything unsaid. Outside, the city noise felt distant, as though the world was holding its breath.

It was impossible to ignore what was happening around them—the growing tension in the streets, the hurried conversations in back rooms, and the soldiers on both sides preparing for something they couldn't yet name.

Titans clash on Holy Day

On October 6, 1973, as Israel observed Yom Kippur, its holiest day—a day when the nation came to a standstill for fasting and prayer—Egyptian and Syrian forces launched a massive coordinated attack.

What many Israelis had believed

was unthinkable became a harsh reality. From the south, Egyptian troops crossed the Suez Canal, storming across the Bar-Lev Line, catching Israeli defenses off-guard. In the north, Syrian tanks and soldiers poured over the Golan Heights, advancing with force and determination.

It wasn't just a military operation—but a calculated strike meant to reclaim lost honor and land. The humiliation of the Six-Day War of 1967, where Israel had seized the Sinai Peninsula, the Golan Heights, Gaza, and the West Bank, still hung heavily over Egypt and Syria. For them, this war was a way to reclaim dignity and territory, and to show that Israel was not untouchable.

In the first days, Israel took heavy losses. Unprepared and caught off-guard, their soldiers scrambled to regroup as Egyptian forces pushed deep into Sinai, and Syrian units made dangerous gains in the north. For a time, it seemed like Israel's worst fears had come true—a multi-front war against better-prepared enemies.

But as the days passed, Israel's military began to recover. Reserves were called up, and counterattacks began. In the Sinai, Israeli troops fought fiercely to push Egyptian forces back from their newly gained positions. In the Golan, Israeli tanks battled Syrian armor, eventually driving them back over the highlands.

Still, the price was high. The battle for the Golan Heights alone was among the fiercest tank battles since

World War II, with massive casualties on both sides.

Behind the scenes, the superpowers were watching — and acting.

■ The United States quickly organized a massive airlift, sending weapons and supplies to Israel to prevent total collapse.

■ The Soviet Union, equally invested, and rushed arms and equipment to Egypt and Syria.

It was more than just a regional fight—it had become a proxy conflict between the two Cold War giants, both trying to influence the balance of power in the Middle East.

But even as the battles raged, another weapon was being prepared — one that didn't fire bullets but would send shockwaves through the world economy. The Arab oil-producing nations, led by Saudi Arabia, decided to use oil as leverage. Furious at Western support for Israel, especially from the U.S., they imposed an oil embargo on countries backing Israel.

Almost overnight, the oil embargo sent fuel prices soaring, leading to shortages, gas lines, and panic in Western nations that depended heavily on Middle Eastern oil. What happened on the battlefields of Sinai and Golan quickly rippled through every gas station in America and Europe.

The war lasted until October 25, 1973, when a UN-brokered ceasefire finally halted the fighting. By that time, Israel had managed to push back both Syrian and Egyptian advances—even crossing the Suez Canal and cutting off parts of the Egyptian Third Army—but the cost was staggering. Thousands were dead, wounded, or missing on all sides.

For Israel, the war shattered the myth of invincibility that had surrounded it since 1967. For Egypt and Syria, while they didn't fully reclaim their lands, they had proven they could challenge Israel and survive—a victory in its own way.

For the rest of the world, the war marked the beginning of a new era, where oil and politics became forever intertwined, and the Middle East would remain at the center of global tensions for years to come.

Sitting there in that smoke-filled room, Dad and Kuser may not have known exactly how it would unfold, but they knew something was coming. Something bigger than anything they had covered before. And when it did, the world would never be the same.

And Dad wrote about all of it. Relentless. Fierce. Unwilling to back down, no matter how dangerous the story. And as the wars raged on, as governments postured and alliances crumbled, his words were there, printed in black and white, telling the world what it didn't want to hear.

A-to-A in High Orbit

Mom's art-based educational program was growing beyond anything she had imagined while Dad was making a name for himself in journalism. What started as a small classroom idea had become an international movement that connected schools across the U.S. and Europe.

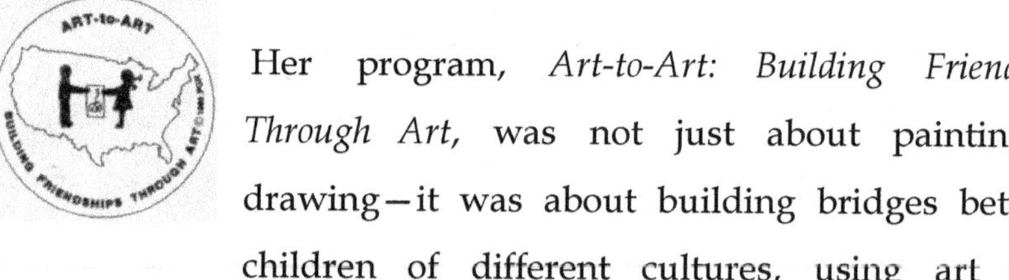

Her program, *Art-to-Art: Building Friendships Through Art*, was not just about painting or drawing—it was about building bridges between children of different cultures, using art as a universal language.

By the time we moved overseas, over 200 U.S. schools were participating, exchanging art projects and letters with schools in countries like France, Germany, England, and even Israel. Students shared their own worldviews through drawings, paintings, and sculptures. The art pieces would travel from school to school, helping kids understand what life looked like in another part of the world.

One evening, I remember walking into the kitchen and finding Mom sitting at the table, sorting through stacks of artwork sent from children across the country. Bright, colorful drawings covered the entire surface—pictures of families, farms, cities, and children holding hands across the globe.

She looked up and smiled when she saw me but quickly returned to carefully wrapping a watercolor in tissue paper.

"You're working late again," I said, sliding into the chair next to her.

"There's always more to do when you're sending children's dreams across the ocean," she replied with a soft laugh.

I picked up one of the drawings. It was a simple image of a boy standing next to a tree, holding his artwork, but what caught my eye was the writing at the bottom, in shaky letters: *"This is me under the tree where I sit alone. But now I will share my monster with big ears painting with friends far away."*

I raised an eyebrow, and before I could say anything, Mom's expression turned more serious — thoughtful, even emotional.

"You know, Benjamin," she began, folding her hands over the table, "that drawing... that's from a boy named *Eli*. He's nine years old. Lives in Indiana. His teachers told me something when they sent me his work."

I tilted my head. "What's that?"

Mom took a deep breath, as though she was still processing the story herself.

"They said Eli had never spoken in class. Never said a word, not even to his classmates. They thought he was mute, maybe traumatized."

I frowned, listening intently.

"But when his teacher announced that the school's art projects would be part of the Art-to-Art exchange, and that some would travel to schools all over the U.S., and even Europe, something in him... shifted," she said, her voice soft but charged with meaning.

She smiled a little, but there was a glisten in her eyes.

"They told me that when Eli found out his drawing might be selected to go on tour and that it could be displayed at the National Annual

'Art-to-Art' provides Montville students with a picture of kids, life in other states

By CHRISTOPHER CHAZIN

206

Site Exhibit, he raised his hand for the first time."

I blinked in surprise. "Seriously? What did he say?"

Mom looked at me for a long moment, as if wanting me to truly understand before she spoke again.

She wiped her eyes quickly before answering.

"He said, 'Will they know it's mine? Will kids far away see my tree?'"

I felt a lump rise in my throat.

Mom nodded. "His teacher told me the whole class just sat there in shock. They'd never heard his voice before. And you know what, Ben?" she added, leaning in a little closer, her hands folding and unfolding. "From that day on, he started talking. First in small sentences, then in full conversations."

"Because of the art project?" I asked, still wrapping my head around it.

"Because he knew he had something to say — and now, people would finally listen," she said.

I leaned back in my chair, glancing again at the boy's drawing, now holding it with a kind of reverence I hadn't before.

"That's... incredible," I whispered.

Mom smiled, though her eyes were still moist. "That's what this is about. It's not just colors on paper. It's giving children a voice—especially the ones who think no one is listening."

She gently patted the stack of drawings. "You see all these? Look at this photo shows. It proves every one of these kids has something to say. And when their art travels, when it reaches other children—suddenly, they're part of something bigger. They're part of a world that sees them."

She sat back in her chair, letting out a slow breath, and looked out the kitchen window, as if seeing beyond our backyard and imagining the places these pieces would travel.

"You know, sometimes we don't realize how much power there is in letting someone share a piece of themselves. It can break walls down that no medicine or therapy ever could," she said, her voice now steady.

She turned back to me with a gentle smile. "That's why I won't stop doing this. Look at this photo. Now you know why I am not for anything. Not even when it keeps me up half the night."

I nodded, realizing for the first time that her program was more than just art. It was hope in the form of paint and pencil.

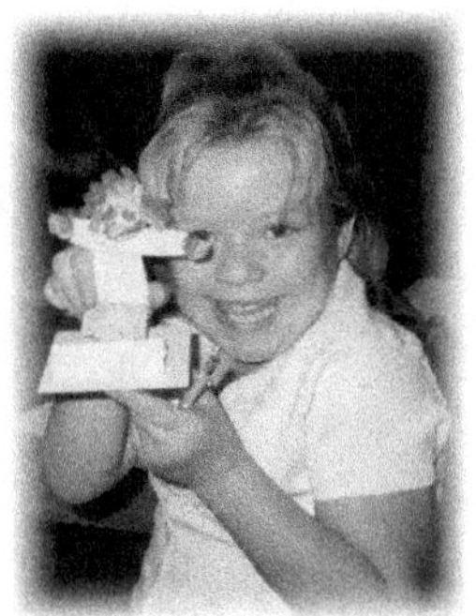

And before I left the kitchen, I glanced one more time at Eli's picture. It wasn't just a monster with big ears anymore. It was the first time he had spoken to the world—and maybe the first time someone was ready to listen.

Bonds of Childhood Friendships

Although I attended an American school during those years, I was deeply exposed to my Jewish heritage.

I favored my Irish mother—crystal blue eyes, white ash blonde hair that shimmered almost silver in the bright sun, and skin that tanned to a dark bronze every summer. Among the children in Jerusalem, where olive skin and dark hair were the norm, I stood out like a lighthouse on a dark coast.

At first, it made me feel out of place. But over time, it became something my friends teased me about—especially Jackie and Bobby Coleman, the children of my father's close colleagues.

From the day we met, we were inseparable. Bobby and I were drawn together by the usual boyish interests — climbing trees, sneaking into abandoned places we weren't supposed to be, and trying to outdo each other in everything from marbles to makeshift soccer matches.

But Jackie was different. She wasn't just another kid in the group. She carried a kind of quiet strength even as a child, and somehow, I always felt like she understood things the rest of us didn't.

Jackie and Bobby lived on a small dairy farm on the outskirts of Jerusalem — something that fascinated me

to no end. Their little piece of farmland felt like another world in a city filled with politics, soldiers, and history on every corner.

One warm spring afternoon, the three of us were

sitting under a large fig tree at the edge of their farm, watching the cows graze lazily under the sun. Jackie tossed pebbles into a small ditch; her sun-streaked brown hair pulled back in a loose ponytail. Bobby was chewing on a piece of straw like he was some kind of cowboy.

"Hey, Ben," Bobby said, squinting at me through the sunlight, "how come you look like a foreign movie star or something?"

I blinked, caught off guard. "What do you mean?"

Jackie smirked but didn't look up. "You know what he means. Nobody around here has hair like yours. It's like... white, but not old man white. And your eyes—" she turned to face me now, studying me as if seeing me for the first time, "—they're like the sky when it's about to storm. Makes you look like you're from somewhere else."

I shifted uncomfortably, pulling at the grass near my feet. "My mom's Irish. Maybe that's why."

Bobby snorted. "Yeah, but you're Jewish too, right? I mean, your dad is."

"Yeah," I said, shrugging. "Nana says I'm both. She says I got the Irish outside and Jewish inside."

Jackie grinned. "Maybe you're part fairy," she teased, tossing a pebble at me playfully.

I laughed. "Maybe."

But then Bobby got serious for a minute. "Still, don't you ever wish you looked like everyone else? You know, so people would stop staring?"

I thought about that. I did wish that, sometimes. Walking through Jerusalem's markets, I always caught people looking at me twice. Even at school, some kids would whisper behind my back.

But before I could answer, Jackie jumped in, her voice sharp in how she got when standing up for someone.

"Why should he?" she said. "So what if he looks different? Maybe he's supposed to."

I looked at her, surprised by the sudden defense.

Bobby raised an eyebrow. "Supposed to? Like what, some kind of hero in a story?"

Jackie shrugged but didn't back down. "Maybe. My mom says some people are born to do something important. Maybe that's why Ben looks different. So people notice when he does something big."

That stuck with me.

I tried to brush it off, but later that night, I kept thinking about her words. What if she was right?

"Dryin' Times on the Farm"

Still, at that age, farming was what really caught my attention, not destiny. Jackie talked about it constantly — how she was going to take over the farm one day, make it even bigger, raise all kinds of animals, and grow vegetables to sell at the market.

"You really like this farm stuff, huh?" I asked her one afternoon as we helped her dad stack bales of hay.

Jackie wiped her forehead with the back of her hand, nodding. "I love it. Being outside, working with animals... making things grow. It's better than being cooped up in some office all day."

Bobby rolled his eyes. "You're gonna smell like cow poop forever."

She smacked him lightly with a handful of hay. "Better than smelling like ink and paper like you will in some boring job."

I grinned, watching them banter. But I also felt a strange sense of connection to what Jackie was saying.

"Maybe I like it too," I said quietly, more to myself than to them. "Maybe there's something about growing stuff... working with my hands."

Jackie looked at me and smiled. "See? Told you it's not just me."

Later that night, as I was helping Mom clear the dishes from dinner, I told her about Jackie's dream of running a farm.

Mom paused, looking at me with those sharp eyes that always seemed to know more than she let on.

"You know, Benjamin," she said softly, "your great-grandfather was a farmer. Maybe that's where it comes from. Maybe it's in your blood, like in hers."

She set down a plate and turned to me.

"And don't forget what your grandmother Marganita told you," she added, her voice quiet but firm. "Someday, you'll meet someone who will change your life forever. Someone who makes you see who you really are."

I stared at her, thinking about Jackie's smile, about the way she always seemed to understand me without me saying a word.

At seven years old, I didn't know what love was. But even then, I knew there was something about Jackie that felt different, something that made me feel... like I belonged.

Bobby was my best friend. But Jackie—she was something more, even if I couldn't explain it.

Back then, I thought Nana's Rune Stones were just old games. But looking back now, I wonder if she already knew what I didn't.

"Maria von Trapp"

Posed Summer of 1972, Trapp Lodge, Stove, Vermont

BACK HOME FOR VACATION

"A man does what he must - in spite of personal consequences, in spite of obstacles and dangers and pressures - and that is the basis of all human morality."
John Fitzgerald Kennedy

$\heartsuit$

It was the early summer of 1973, and I was wrestling with being in my teen years, caught between being a child and something older, though I didn't know what that meant. We also went back to Traverse City-Suttons Bay for a special annual Grabowsky-Cohen-Cohan family reunion that Nana arranged, but still, it would be short for us for the same reasons as before, as Dad's work as a foreign correspondent kept us overseas in Jerusalem. But now stepping back onto American soil felt like breathing again.

Traverse City, perched on the shores of Lake Michigan's Grand Traverse Bay, was as beautiful as I remembered — if not more so. The vast expanse of turquoise water stretched endlessly, its gentle waves lapping the sandy beaches that framed the city. Sailboats and fishing vessels bobbed along the marina, their white sails snapping against the summer breeze.

The air was sweet — not just from the lake, but from

something else — the cherry orchards that ran like ribbons across the hills and valleys beyond the town. Traverse City wasn't just any town; it was the *'Cherry Capital of the World.'* By July, the whole region would transform for the National Cherry Festival, a week-long celebration of that rich agricultural heritage.

Cherry Queen, Traverse City, Michigan

I remembered the smell of cherry pies wafting through the air, the colorful parades, carnival rides, and farmers' markets overflowing with crates of bright red fruit. But this time, we arrived a little before that grand celebration, in the calm before the festival storm.

It was more than just nostalgia that brought us back. Mom sensed something stirring deep in Dad — something restless.

"He was feeling the burn when new becomes old, too much of the same, and I can see it," Mom said softly as she stood by the window of our rented cottage overlooking the bay. Her eyes followed the waves as if they held answers. "Your father is in search of something... something more permanent. He's tired, Ben. Tired of running from war to war. He wants to feel grounded again."

I looked at her, noting the way her fingers lightly gripped the edge of the curtain, as though holding onto something invisible.

And she was right. I could see it in Dad's face—that hunger for home. After years of life overseas—shifting between hotels, embassies, and war zones—there was a hollowness behind his eyes, like a man craving the comfort of the familiar, the steady routine, the pace of a small-town life, one of camaraderie and they greet each other by first name.

They had always dreamed of returning to the place where their life began—to the city where they spent their honeymoon, where Dad first cut his teeth as a young reporter for the 𝕿𝖗𝖆𝖛𝖊𝖗𝖘𝖊 𝕮𝖎𝖙𝖞 𝕻𝖔𝖘𝖙.

As soon as we arrived, the town embraced us like family, and my parents began making the rounds—visiting old friends, neighbors, and family who had stayed behind. Mom rekindled friendships over coffee, while relatives filled our ears with stories about how much had changed—and how much had stayed exactly the same.

But while Mom and I made the rounds of family reunions and coffee chats, Dad seemed to move on a different current.

One morning, after a long breakfast with the family—where my uncles argued over politics and the women swapped recipes—Dad stood abruptly, smoothing down his shirt.

"I'm going for a walk," he said, though we all knew what that meant.

Mom just gave a small smile and nodded. "Go on, Nathan," she said, her voice soft but knowing.

I watched him walk away, a thin man with a strong stride, heading down the street that would take him toward the center of town.

But he wasn't just wandering.

Later that day, I heard Mom on the phone with Aunt Esther, her voice hushed but excited.

"Yes, Nathan went to the *Post*," she said, laughing gently. "You know, he always said that's where he truly learned what it means to be a journalist."

As I listened from the kitchen doorway, she turned slightly and caught my eye, giving me a quiet smile.

"You know, Ben, your father has always dreamed

of running a paper like that," she said when she hung up the phone. "Something small enough to care about the people, but big enough to tell real stories — not just politics and war."

I thought about that as I walked along the beach later, the soft crunch of sand under my feet, the lake wind tugging at my shirt.

I knew that Dad had seen too much in his time abroad — wars, revolutions, lives torn apart. Maybe this small city, with its cherry orchards, calm bay, and close-knit community, was what he needed to feel whole again.

As I glanced out over the sparkling water, watching children run along the shore and couples walk hand in hand, I realized why Traverse City had always been their dream.

Here, life moved slower, measured by seasons of cherries, summer tourists, and gentle waves, not by bombs, gunfire, or political coups.

By the time we returned to Traverse City in 1973, Murray Bernard was running the *Post* like a well-oiled machine, and the paper was thriving beyond anyone's expectations.

Over the last five years, the *Post* had tripled in size, growing from a small-town daily to a regional powerhouse. The paper now averaged 24 pages every weekday, but on Sundays, it became a massive edition that quadrupled in size, packed with features, special columns, and expanded advertising.

Even more impressive was how circulation had doubled, especially during the tourist season when visitors flooded into Traverse City for the National Cherry Festival and summer lake vacations. Tourists wanted to know what was happening around town, and Murray made sure the *Post* had everything—from local events and community stories to state and national headlines.

But Murray wasn't stopping there. The commercial printing operation was booming at the *Post* as well. Small businesses, resorts, and regional advertisers turned to Murray's paper for everything from custom brochures and flyers to event posters. His printing presses ran day and night, keeping up with demand.

It was in this high-energy environment that Dad went to visit Murray—and as Mom later put it, "Murray was going full guns."

As Dad described it to me, Murray greeted him like an old friend the moment he walked into the busy newsroom. The two men had known each other since Dad's earliest days as a reporter, and over the years, their relationship had grown from mentor and apprentice to something like brothers.

"Murray was always more than just a boss to me, Ben," Dad told me years later. "He was like the older brother I never had. He showed me how to be tough when I needed to be but never forget the people behind the story."

As they sat in Murray's glass-walled office overlooking the bustling newsroom, Murray got right to the point.

"Listen, Nathan," Murray said, leaning forward on his desk, his sleeves rolled up, as if he had just come from the press room. "I bought a paper over in Eagle River, Wisconsin—a resort town, with good growth potential. But it needs someone like you to turn it into something real. I don't want a clone of the Post. I want someone to take what we've built here and make it their own. New ideas, fresh energy—someone hungry."

Dad told me later, "It wasn't just about managing a newspaper, Ben. Murray was handing me a blank canvas and saying, *'Go paint something.'*"

With a smile, Dad added, "He tossed me that opportunity like a bone, just like Kuser did back in Jerusalem, but this time it was here—home."

Murray knew Dad well. They had spent long hours together over the years, working late on breaking stories, hashing out editorials, and even talking about life outside the newsroom. That bond went beyond business—it was built on respect and trust, the kind that only forms between two men who've been through the same fires and know each other's strengths and faults.

But despite the excitement of the offer, it was time for Mom and me to return to Jerusalem, while Dad was leaving the next day, going directly to cover the growing unrest in the West Bank. Dad also needed time to consider Murray's job offer and he wasn't about to make a decision without Mom. She had built her own career—her Art-to-Art education program was thriving—and any big change would affect all of us.

So the next night, Dad picked up the phone from our rented Sutton Bag cottage and called Mom in Jerusalem. I can still imagine him sitting on the edge of the bed, the room quiet except for the hum of the line, waiting for her to answer.

When she finally picked up, I heard later that there was a long pause after he told her about Murray's offer—a pause so thick, it felt like both sides of the world were holding their breath.

Then, in her steady, calm voice, Mom gave him her answer—the kind of answer that didn't need a second thought.

"Go for it, Nathan," she said warmly. "I'm ready to come home." With Mom's support Dad said, "I called

Murray from the West Bank and asked him if his offer still stands."

"Huh. Didn't I tell you I am ready when you are," said Murray. "When can you start?"

"Yesterday, but I might need at least a month, considering I currently don't live around the block," said Dad.

"Your office will be ready at the Daily Review. Welcome home my friend," said Murray.

Years later, when Dad would retell the story, usually with a soft chuckle, he always said, "I can still hear her voice like it was yesterday. She didn't even hesitate.

And when she said she was ready, that's when I knew it was time to stop searching."

Before Mom and I returned to American soil for good, Dad was settled in his new role as Editor and Publisher of the *Daily Review* in Eagle River, Wisconsin, a small but promising paper in need of a fresh vision. Next on his agenda was finding a family home and Dad was never one to settle for just any house—he wanted something that felt like it belonged to us, something that could be a permanent home after years of moving and temporary places.

When he first met Edward Welch, the local real

estate agent, Dad made it clear what he was looking for.

"Something solid. Something with character. Not one of those cookie-cutter places," he told Welch.

Welch, a thin man with a neat mustache and the calm manner of someone who knew the town like the back of his hand, leaned back in his chair, thinking for a moment.

"Well, there's a place that's about to hit the market," Welch said, tapping his pen on the desk. "Big house, lots of land. Needs a lot of work, though—more than most folks are willing to take on. Honestly, Nathan, it's a bit of a mess."

Dad leaned forward, his eyes already alive with interest. "Tell me more."

Welch described the house in broad strokes—a large, old estate home with creaky floorboards, peeling paint, and a roof that had seen better days. But underneath all that, he said, was a place with history, strong bones, and enough land for a real family home.

"It's gonna take a lot of elbow grease, Mr.

Grabowsky," Welch warned. "But if you've got the patience, you won't find anything like it for the price."

That was all Dad needed to hear.

"With some hard work and a little TLC, sounds like the kind of place I'm looking for," Dad replied without missing a beat.

Welch agreed to meet him later that day at 5:00 p.m. at the *Daily Review* office, so Dad could settle into the newsroom before heading out to see the property.

What Welch didn't know was that Dad wasn't just looking for a house—he was looking for a place to plant roots, to give us the kind of home he and Mom had dreamed of while living in war-torn cities abroad.

Honey, The Dream is Over

Since Mom and I were still living in Jerusalem at the time, Dad had to telephone us about the house he had found. I can still remember that evening, sitting at the small table in our apartment as Mom answered the phone, her eyes brightening as Dad described every corner of the house with excitement in his voice.

As she listened, her face lit up like a lantern in the dark, and by the time she hung up, her cheeks were flushed with excitement. I knew without her saying a word—this was the home she had always dreamed of.

Even though I was their only child, she had always said she wanted a big house, a place that could hold not just us but all the extended family—a home filled with noise, laughter, and life. "A home should be big enough to hold love in every room," she used to say, often while running her fingers across old family photos.

I suppose she had been searching for a place to settle, much like Dad, after so many years of living between foreign places, moving with the uncertainty of Dad's career.

And as an American folk singer Joan Baez once said, *"As long as one keeps searching, the answers will come."*

It felt almost like fate that nearly 14 years after their wedding, they would finally find a home that echoed the place where their married life had begun—the *Manor on the Lake* in Green River, Wisconsin, where they had honeymooned. Dad said this new house reminded him so much of that inn; it was like stepping back into time. An almost perfect clone, but rural and without the lake, he called it—except this one would be ours, to own and build a future in.

The property was breathtaking. Set in the rolling countryside on 200 acres of lush, green horse and dairy farm, the land stretched as far as the eye could see, dotted with groves of trees and wide-open pastures. To the west lay the American Legion State Forest, a dense wall of towering pines and oaks that seemed to guard the property. To the east, the Nicolet National Forest offered miles of untouched wilderness. And all around were lakes, sparkling under the sun, scattered like pieces of glass about ten miles south of the main town of Eagle River, Wisconsin.

At the center of it all, perched on the highest hill as if watching over the land, was the house—a grand, four-story structure that looked like it had stepped out of a novel.

It had once been a luxurious Bed and Breakfast Inn, a place where wealthy visitors from Milwaukee and Chicago would escape to in the summer, seeking rest and privacy in its elegant halls.

The house itself was enormous, unlike anything I had ever seen in real life. Twenty bedrooms, each with tall windows that let the sunlight pour in, and eight full bathrooms with claw-foot tubs and vintage fixtures that looked like something out of a history book.

You walked into a giant foyer with a spiral staircase, winding like something from *Gone With the Wind*, leading all the way to the fourth floor. Two massive living rooms, each one large enough to hold all of our extended family with room to spare. There was a dining room so big Dad joked you could play basketball in it—and he wasn't far off.

The kitchen was equally grand—a huge eat-in space with a wide hearth and a pantry the size of a garage, enough to store food for an army. A library and a den, with shelves built into the walls, held echoes of a time when people would gather around to read and talk instead of watching TV.

And then there were the special rooms. A billiard room that, as Dad laughed, "would make Minnesota Fats himself jealous," and a family room with a fireplace so big Dad said, "Santa could ride his sleigh right down and still have room for the reindeer."

The basement was a world of its own—complete with a wine cellar, and an underground passage leading to the barns, which I imagined were used when the winter snows got too heavy to walk above ground.

Outside, broad wrap-around porches framed the house, perfect for sitting on long summer evenings. Tall colonial columns supported the porch roofs, and green canvas canopies shaded every window, giving the house a stately but welcoming look.

When Mom heard all this from Dad, she didn't hesitate. "Nathan," she said softly, "if you believe this is the home we're meant to have, then let's make it ours."

So it was only a matter of a few weeks when we returned to the US from Jerusalem, for a new chapter, far away from the wars and tensions we had lived with for years.

But with new beginnings also came change.

About a year after we settled, Grandpapa Asa passed away, leaving a hole in our family. Nana moved in with us, armed with her sharp wit, strong opinions, and fierce, tender love for family. She was a woman of deep traditions, and she threw herself into managing the house as if it were her personal mission.

"Nana always believed that a family should gather under one roof," Mom said one evening, watching Nana bustle around the kitchen preparing for another family gathering. "Now she has the space to make that happen."

For Nana, this house was more than just walls and rooms—it was a place to continue family traditions, host reunions, and keep everyone connected.

For me, though, adjusting to this new life was harder. I was nearly 15, caught between the world I had left behind in Jerusalem and this vast new world of forests and farms.

Though I tried to write to my friends from overseas, my letters became fewer and fewer as the months passed, and eventually, they stopped altogether. It was as though I was trying to hold onto a piece of a life that no longer fit, like clothes I had outgrown.

Dad, seeing how much I missed my old life, let me call my friends occasionally, but even those conversations became harder as time went on.

Instead, I began focusing on something else — working the land, learning everything I could from Dottie and Roger, who owned a neighboring farm. They taught me how to care for animals, plant crops, and fix fences, and soon, I found myself drawn to the hard, honest work of farming, something that made sense in a way the rest of my life didn't.

As I built my own small farm projects, tending animals and growing vegetables, I found a kind of peace in the routine of caring for living things.

And though my thoughts of the Middle East and my childhood friends would sometimes creep in during quiet moments, I pushed them aside. I needed to focus on the life in front of me — the fields, the animals, and the family that now filled our enormous home.

In time, the house became more than just a building — it became a living, breathing part of our family, holding our losses, dreams, and hopes within its walls.

And maybe, as Nana would say, it was always meant to be that way — a place where new roots would finally take hold.

"Aging Beauty"

FLOWS OF CHANGE 1976-1980

"Two such as you with such a master speed, cannot be parted nor be swept away,
from one another once you are agreed, that life is only life forevermore,
together wing to wing and oar to oar."

Robert Frost, Limes from The Master Speed (1934)

♥

My 15th birthday landed right in the heart of our annual Thanksgiving and family reunion, a tradition so deeply rooted in our household that everything—meals, stories, and music—seemed to orbit around it. But this year wasn't just about turning fifteen. It was also the moment where two sides of my heritage met: I received my Roman Catholic confirmation and my Jewish Bar Mitzvah.

The ceremony wasn't flashy. It was deeply personal. The priest and the rabbi both agreed to a small, private service that reflected our family's respect for faith on both sides. Nana cried during the Hebrew prayers. My mother lit candles with shaky hands. My father looked proud but distant, like he was trying to understand how I had come to stand between two worlds with such ease.

Yet it wasn't just the dual rite of passage that

made this gathering different.

I had grown into something more than just a curious teenager. Over the past year, I had thrown myself headfirst into working the land. And now, with soil under my fingernails and calluses on my palms, I had something to show for it.

That afternoon, just before dinner, I lined the kitchen table with glass jars and baskets full of the work I had poured myself into all season: thick red tomato juice, shiny Bread and Butter pickles, peas, string beans, corn cut straight from the cob, and my proudest crop—massive, chemical-free Idaho-sized potatoes that filled a wooden crate to the top.

I didn't say anything at first. I just waited for someone to notice.

My cousin Jeff Jones popped open a jar and whistled. "Did you really make all this?" he asked, holding up a pickle slice.

I nodded. "Grew, picked, canned. All of it."

My dad, standing at the head of the kitchen, folded his arms and stepped closer. He examined the spread like an editor reading a fresh draft.

"These tomatoes," he said, lifting one of the jars, "you grew them from seed?"

"From seed. No pesticides. I used a composting method Nana taught me. Just soil, sun, and water."

He glanced at me, a curious light in his eyes. "And you did all the canning yourself?"

"With Nana's help on the first few rounds," I replied, "but after that, it was all me."

He looked impressed—genuinely impressed—and that meant more than any applause.

As the rest of the family trickled in, word of my harvest spread through the house faster than the smell of roasted turkey and spiced apple cider.

Cheating on a piece of string bean, Uncle Johnny raised his eyebrows. "These beans are the real deal. You could sell this stuff."

Aunt Jeanie was already asking for my pickling recipe, and Nana hovered nearby, whispering to anyone who'd listen, "He's got your great-grandfather's touch. I knew it."

That night's meal was a true fusion of generations and cultures. My fresh, homegrown dishes were served alongside the usual holiday staples and an ethnic spread that represented every branch of our tree—potato latkes, stuffed cabbage, pierogies, Irish soda bread, brisket, and sweet kugel. Every bite felt like it came with a story.

After dinner, with plates cleared and dessert underway, Uncle Oscar Stone stood up and tapped his glass. He wasn't one for long speeches, but the room fell quiet this time.

"I've been assigned to a new project," he announced. "IBM wants me to oversee the installation of a new computer system at the Foreign Ministry of Justice in Jerusalem."

The room buzzed with soft murmurs.

He continued, "It's going to be a long-term assignment. Four years, minimum. And I'll be training their internal staff once the system's in place."

Aunt Esther looked less thrilled. She leaned forward, arms crossed. "The girls are going into high school," she said, glancing at Joyce Marie and Carol Ann, who sat stiffly beside her. "This means they'll miss dances, pep rallies, prom... the whole American high school experience."

"They'll gain something better," Uncle Oscar replied calmly. "They'll gain perspective. They'll meet people from different cultures, learn to think differently. It's not just a job. It's a family opportunity."

Carol Ann raised her hand awkwardly as if she were still in school. "Will we still have American classes?"

"You'll attend an international school," Oscar said, "English instruction, U.S. curriculum. And you'll still graduate with a U.S. diploma."

Joyce Marie muttered under her breath, "Do they have malls in Jerusalem?"

That got a laugh out of the adults. Aunt Esther sighed, then gave in with a half-smile. "I guess the multicultural experience might do them some good."

Nana chimed in from the corner, always ready with a reminder from the past. "When Asa and I came here, we had nothing but a trunk and a prayer. You'll have a full house and a salary. Go. Learn. Bring those lessons back."

Uncle Oscar raised his glass. "To new beginnings. And to Benjamin—for feeding us like a seasoned farmer."

Everyone clinked glasses and took sips of wine or cider. I sat quietly, not sure how to take in all the attention, but proud—really proud—that the food on their plates had come from my own hands.

Later that night, Dad leaned over to me while I was loading plates into the sink.

"You know," he said quietly, "you've got more discipline at fifteen than I had at twenty-five."

I looked at him, surprised.

"You think this is worth keeping at?" I asked.

He nodded. "People talk a lot about purpose. Most never find it. But when your hands are in the dirt and your head's full of plans—that's something real. Keep going."

And I did.

After the family had settled into their after-dinner lull, the house had that soft, warm buzz that only came after a meal shared by dozens of people who all somehow connected back to the same tree. Plates were stacked high, dessert had made its rounds twice, and the older adults were now drifting toward the den, drawn to the familiar hum of coffee pots and murmured conversation.

I made my way outside to the porch. The air was cold enough to remind you it was late November, but it was not biting. The stars above were bright, free from city lights. I was leaning against the railing, staring out at the yard where some of the younger cousins were still running around with jackets half-zipped, when I heard the screen door creak open behind me.

"Mind if I join you?"

I turned. It was Carol Ann, a half-smirk on her face and hands stuffed in the pockets of a tan corduroy jacket.

"Always," I said with a grin, scooting over to make room.

She plopped down beside me, her long legs stretching out in front of her. Even in the moonlight, the sharp angle of her jaw and those unmistakable crystal blue eyes caught the light just right. It was hard to believe this was the same awkward, wiry girl who used to run around with tape on her glasses and scabs on both knees.

According to family legend, Carol Ann was the younger of the twins—by ten minutes. Aunt Esther used to say she didn't want to come out, that she made the doctor wait, as if the world had to meet Joyce Marie first before she'd consider showing up. But once she found her footing, Carol Ann turned out to be the one who charged forward—never afraid to climb the tallest tree, sneak into the attic after dark, or say something outrageous in a room full of serious grownups.

Now, at fifteen, she'd stretched out tall and lean, with golden blonde hair that curled slightly at the ends, like it was teasing the air. Her frame was all limbs and elegance, even if she still carried that edge of mischief in the way she spoke.

"So," she started, nudging my shoulder, "Mr. Farmer Boy of the North—what's next? Planning to run a cucumber empire?"

I laughed. "Funny. Thought I'd go global with potatoes first. Spud domination."

She snorted, then tossed her head back with a laugh. "God, I missed this."

"Missed what?"

"This," she gestured between us, "you and me. Laughing over dumb stuff while Joyce Marie sits inside practicing her Miss Universe answers."

That made me chuckle. "Is she still giving you that death glare every time you breathe near her?"

"She hasn't stopped since we were six," Carol Ann replied. "I moved her hairbrush this morning—just shifted it an inch. She acted like I'd committed a federal offense."

"Classic Joyce," I said. "Remember the marshmallow incident?"

She gasped. "When we stuffed her pillow with Peeps? How could I forget? She screamed like she'd been attacked by a sugar monster."

"You blamed it on the cat."

"Which we didn't even own," she grinned.

Our laughter echoed through the cold air, catching on the wind. It was always like this between us—easy, sharp, light. Carol Ann and I had grown into this quiet understanding that we could say anything, joke about everything, and never have to explain ourselves. She got it. She got me.

After a moment of quiet, she tilted her head and looked at me.

"You know," she said more softly, "you've changed."

"How so?"

"You seem... grounded. Not that you weren't before. But this whole thing with the farm, the vegetables, the canning—" she paused, "—you've kind of figured out who you are, haven't you?"

I shrugged. "Maybe. I just like doing something that feels real. Growing stuff. Feeding people. It makes sense to me."

She nodded, chewing on her bottom lip like she was weighing a thought.

"I think that's what scares me," she said finally. "This move to Jerusalem. Everything I know is here. And I don't know who I am there."

That hit differently. The playfulness in her tone had dropped. This was the real Carol Ann—the one who could crack a joke one second and go deep the next.

"You'll be fine," I said quietly. "You're braver than you think."

She looked at me, searching. "You really believe that?"

"Yeah," I said. "I've seen you climb a windmill with a busted ankle and walk across the top like it was nothing. You'll figure it out. Besides… they've got trees in Jerusalem. You'll feel at home." That made her smile again.

Just then, the screen door opened again. Joyce Marie stepped out, wrapped in a heavy wool shawl, holding a mug of tea like a queen surveying her kingdom.

"Oh great," she muttered, seeing us. "The mischievous duo plotting world chaos again."

"Only your world," Carol Ann replied without missing a beat.

Joyce gave us the kind of look that only big sisters can perfect—equal parts annoyance and exhausted acceptance—before turning around and going back inside.

"Still think she's the pretty one?" I asked, nudging Carol Ann again.

Carol grinned. "Let her have the beauty pageants. I'll be the one living in a villa with a vineyard and a cow sanctuary."

"Don't forget your cucumber empire," I added.

She laughed again, louder this time. And in that moment, I realized just how much I was going to miss her when she left.

We sat there for a while longer, letting the cold air numb our fingers as our breath turned to clouds.

Eventually, she stood and looked down at me. "Don't get too famous while I'm gone," she said, brushing a leaf off her coat.

"No promises," I said with a wink.

She leaned in and hugged me—quick but tight—and then disappeared back inside, leaving behind the scent of apple pie and wood smoke in her wake.

Inside, the warmth of the house welcomed me back from the porch. Laughter rolled down the hall from the den where most of the adults had gathered. The scent of cinnamon and baked apples still hung in the air. As I passed the dining room, I heard Dad and Uncle Oscar deep in conversation. Dad was recounting a moment from his days in Jerusalem—something about a sudden curfew and a half-finished story that ended up making the front page in Tel Aviv and Cairo.

But I didn't stop. I headed straight for the kitchen, where Nana was holding court, standing next to my jars of preserved vegetables like they were museum pieces.

"I tell you," she was saying to Aunt Esther, "these spuds reminded me of my papa's crops. Big as a man's fist and clean as temple linens. You remember I told you about my father's farm?"

Esther nodded, clearly entertained, even though she had heard the story before. I smiled and leaned on the doorframe.

Nana turned to me, eyes twinkling. "Benjamin, do you know how your great-grandfather used to mulch? No machines. Just horse manure, grass, leaves—anything the land gave back. And the worms! Oh, they loved him."

"Worms have good taste," I said with a smirk.

She laughed, reaching over to squeeze my arm. "Papa used to line us kids up on weekends with baskets of vegetables, and we'd sell them by the roadside. Peddling turnips and onions like they were gold." She paused and gave me a look filled with quiet pride. "You've got his hands, you know. His rhythm."

Before I could answer, Dad strolled in, hearing just enough to jump in.

"Ya know Mama," he said, plucking a piece of pickle from a jar, "I read somewhere that genes can skip a generation or two."

Nana raised a brow, crossing her arms. "Or maybe it just takes the right soul to call them back."

I stayed quiet, watching them with a sense of stillness. I didn't always know what to make of Nana's spiritual talk, but a part of me wanted to believe when she said things like that.

Over the next four years, I wasn't just growing crops—I was growing into a kind of clarity.

By sixteen, I had become what I often joked was a "part-time student, full-time farmer." I spent my mornings tending to rows of vegetables, afternoons feeding and milking the cows, and evenings reading technical manuals or attending Ag seminars on rotational planting or low-impact irrigation.

What started as a backyard project became a 20-acre operation—10 acres of vegetables, and 10 acres of fruit trees and bushes, still young but already producing enough to keep me busy and my customers loyal.

I named my small business the *Brookside Marketplace II*, in honor of my great-grandfather's original stand, a name that made Nana beam every time she heard it.

I didn't need chemicals or massive machinery. I believed in letting the land do what it was born to do. I layered mulch by hand—leaves, clippings, kitchen scraps—and trusted the worms and microbes to take it from there.

My goal wasn't to be trendy or "'green'." I just didn't want the burden of costs, chemicals, or debt. Nature already had its own system — I just learned how to work with it.

Dad watched me closely during those years — not in a controlling way — but from a distance, as if he were measuring the lines of a story still being written.

I knew he worried about me spreading myself too thin. After all, I was still finishing high school, and he had enrolled me two years earlier in college-level courses at the University of Wisconsin–Rhinelander branch. His goal wasn't to push, but to test my balance.

He never said it outright, but I could tell he didn't want me to fall into something and burn out before I had the chance to really build something meaningful.

I didn't resent it. In fact, I appreciated it. I had room to grow, but never room to coast.

Every holiday, the house was filled with relatives. The reunion had become a set fixture in everyone's calendar — so dependable that even our younger cousins started calling it "Second Christmas."

And every year, Nana brought out her Rune Stones.

It was a ritual. After dinner, after dessert, and after her two glasses of blackberry wine, she would light a small candle, sit at the edge of the table, and empty her worn velvet pouch onto the cloth surface.

"Benjamin, come here," she'd say. "Let's see what's ahead."

I'd humor her, sit down, and smile, watching the stones roll across the fabric in shapes and patterns that I couldn't understand.

She'd speak in that slow, deliberate tone of hers. "Ah... Gebo. The gift again. Always returning to you."

I'd nod, trying not to dismiss it, but still half-lost in the logic of it all. I respected her — but I was rooted in results, in data, in things I could measure. Worms work because they aerate the soil. Compost enriches the ground. Cows give milk if they're healthy. That was my world.

But something about her readings still gave me a kind of strange comfort. Not because I believed in fate, but because she believed in me.

One evening, after most of the family had gone to bed, I found her sitting alone in the kitchen, turning one of the Runes over in her fingers.

"You always pretend like you're not listening," she said without looking up.

"I listen," I replied, sitting across from her.

"You just don't believe."

I thought for a second. "It's not that I don't believe. I just don't understand what I'm supposed to do with it."

She placed the Rune down and met my gaze.

"You already are doing it," she said simply.

And just like that, I knew she wasn't talking about farming, or soil, or vegetables.

She was talking about the way I'd made room in my life for old wisdom and new methods. For faith and facts. For Irish and Jewish. For planting things that would last longer than me.

And maybe, even if I hadn't seen it yet, the Runes were just another way of showing me what I already knew.

Rune	Meaning	Rune	Meaning
Fehu	Abundance, luck, hope, prosperity, wealth, fortune.	Pertho	Mysteries, fortune, chance, mysticism, unknown.
Uruz	Strength, endurance, health, courage, vigor, force.	Algiz	Guardians, defense, instincts, courage, awakenings.
Thurisaz	Challenges, danger, protection, strength, attacks.	Sowilo	Success, vitality, joy, justice, happiness, inspiration.
Ansuz	Revelation, visions, insight, signs, communication.	Tiwaz	Leadership, victory, honor, bravery, courage.
Raidho	Progress, movement, journeys, traveling, evolution.	Berkana	Fertility, renewal, growth, creation, creativity.
Kauna	Enlightenment, insight, knowledge, insight, calling.	Ehwaz	Movement, loyalty, friendship, assistance, animal.
Gebo	Generosity, gift, charity, partnership, service, assistance.	Mannaz	Collective, values, community, relationships.
Wunjo	Pleasure, joy, feasting, celebrations, festivity, success.	Laguz	Water, intuition, dream, imagination, healing, instinct.
Hagalaz	Destruction, wrath of nature, force, testing, change.	Ingwaz	Virility, inner growth, virtue, peace, harmony.
Nauthiz	Need, restriction, resistance, survival, agreements.	Dagaz	Awakening, clarity, consciousness, balance, growth.
Isaz	Suspension, delay, blocks, stillness, waiting, pausing.	Othala	Legacy, inheritance, abundance, values, family.
Jera	Year, endings beginnings, harvest, abundance, learning	Wyrd (optional)	No answer is revealed, secret, mystery.
Eihwaz	Connection, divinity, inspiration, protection.		

"Home Again"

A Heart's Icon

Home again not too far away,

Memories of thy youth glide smoothly like a sleigh.

Rising dawn is painted with a white crispness of a cold air fog,

Trees wearing its winter's dress seemingly in leapfrog,

As I travel the whining roads along the river Mohican,

Weathered by age, the old barn is my beacon.

Holiday wreath with its red fins visually addressing,

Home again gifts thy its bountiful of blessings.

Ben Rayman

THE REUNION-1980

"The family. We were a strange little band of characters trudging through life sharing diseases and toothpaste, coveting one another's desserts, hiding shampoo, borrowing money, locking each other out of our rooms, inflicting pain and kissing to heal it in the same instant, loving, laughing, defending, and trying to figure out the common thread that bound us all together."

Erma Bombeck

The day before Thanksgiving, the house stirred before sunrise. The kitchen was alive with movement—pie crusts chilling, pans clattering, Nana humming in low, deliberate tones as she prepped her cranberry-orange glaze like it was a sacred ritual.

It wasn't chaos. It was controlled anticipation.

Uncle Oscar and his family were finally coming home.

Four years is a long time—especially for teenagers. Carol Ann and Joyce Marie had left as girls. Now, they were arriving as young women who had lived overseas, attended international schools, and seen things most of us only read about in the papers.

The house had been buzzing with their return for weeks. Extra linens were stacked on chairs, old bedrooms reassembled, and photos of the cousins were placed with care on mantels and shelves — as if to make up for lost time.

By mid-afternoon, a light snow had started to fall.

I stood at the window in the front parlor, watching the flakes collect on the porch railing. The driveway was salted and clear, and fresh logs crackled in the fireplace. There was something about this year's reunion that felt deeper — not just festive, but reflective.

The world had kept shifting while Oscar and his family were away. Turmoil in the Middle East. Tension at home. Gas lines. Economic questions. But in this house, things had a way of pausing — just enough for the family to remember what really mattered.

Around three o'clock, the sound of tires crunching gravel broke the quiet.

"Car's here!" someone shouted from the kitchen.

I stepped away from the window just as Nana brushed past me, wiping her hands on a towel, cheeks glowing with the kind of joy that comes from something you've waited too long to feel again.

Uncle Oscar was the first through the door, looking broader in the shoulders and just a little more tired in the eyes. His tie was crooked, but his smile was full.

"Home," he said simply.

Dad was right behind me, already wrapping his older brother in a half-hug and clap on the back. "Took you long enough."

"Not my fault," Oscar laughed. "Try getting through O'Hare with two teenagers, eight suitcases, and a bag of customs paperwork."

Aunt Esther followed next, regal as ever, in a long wool coat, her hair tucked neatly beneath a patterned scarf. She moved with that familiar mix of grace and calculation, eyes already scanning the house as if doing inventory of what had changed.

And then came the twins.

Carol Ann breezed in like she owned the place—bag slung over one shoulder, earbuds tucked into her coat pocket, chin lifted with the kind of confidence that hadn't been there when she left at eleven.

"Okay, who's hugging me first?" she asked, arms already out.

I stepped up without hesitation, and she wrapped me in a tight, two-armed hug that nearly knocked the wind out of me.

"Look at you," she said, pulling back and scanning me. "You've gone full farm-boy. Is that flannel? You're like a catalog."

I grinned. "You're not exactly the awkward kid in glasses anymore."

She gave me a wink. "I told you I'd grow into my elbows."

Then came Joyce Marie—quiet, poised, and still somehow managing to look like she had just stepped out of a magazine. Her coat was neatly belted, her boots polished, not a strand of hair out of place.

She offered a soft smile and leaned in for a brief but polite hug. "You look well, Benny."

"Thanks," I said. "So do you."

She gave a gentle nod, then moved to greet the others, already syncing into the adult conversations like she never left.

Carol Ann lingered near me, watching her sister with a mixture of affection and thinly veiled amusement.

"She's been like that since the embassy dinner," she whispered. "One speech, and suddenly she's royalty."

"You say that like you didn't enjoy it."

"Oh, I loved it," she said with a mischievous grin. "I just didn't let it turn me into a mannequin."

I laughed as we made our way toward the living room, where more greetings were being exchanged, coats were being pulled off, and voices filled the space in layers of welcome.

Nana pulled Uncle Oscar in for a hug that seemed to melt years off both of them. "Now that you're within driving distance, I expect to see you more than once every election cycle."

Oscar kissed her on the cheek. "You'll get tired of me fast."

"Never," Nana said. "And you brought the girls back. That's enough to make the house whole again."

The room settled into a kind of harmony as stories started flowing — what Jerusalem was like, who had grown the most, who was now taller than whom. I drifted to the back corner, plate in hand, listening more than speaking.

For a moment, I thought about the years we'd lost — the holidays they missed, the birthdays we only celebrated over mailed cards and transatlantic phone calls.

I thought about how some people in our lives never quite leave, even when time and distance try to wear the edges of memory down. Some people just stay tucked in the seams, waiting for the right moment to walk back in.

And something in me knew — this reunion wasn't just about family coming home. Something was about to return. Something — or someone — I had tried to forget.

I didn't know yet what that would feel like. But it was close. I could feel it moving beneath the surface like roots under thawing soil.

The door hadn't closed all the way behind them.

There was one more still to arrive.

The last of the snow had started to settle, dusting the porch steps in a thin white film. The door creaked open slightly, letting in a cold wind and a hush of night. Most of the family had moved toward the den, gathered around warm drinks, and shared stories. The heat of the fireplace painted soft glows across their faces.

I returned to the foyer to help Uncle Oscar carry in the final bags, when I heard Nana's voice from the kitchen—not loud, but clear, as if she knew exactly when to speak.

"She's here," she said.

Oscar looked up, pausing mid-step.

The door opened wider, and for a moment, the house seemed to pause—just long enough for the cold to settle in the corners of the room. And then, she stepped through.

There she was.

Jackie Coleman.

The moment cracked open something in me I didn't realize had been sealed. It had been years—four, to be exact—since the Jerusalem sandstorm that took her from view, swallowed by time and distance. I hadn't seen her since I was a boy. And yet, I recognized her instantly. Not by the details of her face, but by the feeling that hit me in the chest like a gust of warm air after a long winter.

She stood just past the threshold, snowflakes clinging to the shoulders of her navy wool coat. She had an ultra-thin figure, still and composed, with a posture that gave her the presence of someone twice her age. Her dark brunette hair cascaded past her shoulders, slightly curled from the cold. Her skin held a natural glow—a cameo-like softness—and her large brown eyes scanned the room with quiet calculation, not fear, just a gentle curiosity. Eyes that didn't search the room. They scanned it—like she was looking for someone.

There was a grace in the way she moved, but it was not staged. She walked with the natural glide of someone unaware of her own elegance—her steps silent, but sure, as if the world owed her a clear path. And despite her silence, something in her carriage gave off almost regal energy—not the kind born from wealth or royalty, but from something more rooted. Composure. Purpose. Poise.

She removed her gloves slowly, adjusting the strap on her shoulder bag. Then she looked up.

Her eyes met Dad's first. They studied one another for a moment before his brow lifted slightly, recognition flickering across his face.

"You said you're from Ramallah?" he asked, stepping forward, his tone easy, warm.

Jackie nodded. "Just outside of it. On the hills."

Dad narrowed his eyes, curious now. "What section of Jerusalem were you near?"

"We moved often," she said. "But toward the end, I was staying near Sheikh Jarrah. Close to the bureau." Then she added with a small smile, "I used to help Sarah's brother's team with translations sometimes. Oscar's Arabic needed a little... backup."

Dad chuckled. "Sounds about right." He tilted his head. "You ever meet a couple named Edward and Victoria Coleman?"

Her eyes lit up like a match to dry cedar. Her breath caught, and then she stepped forward as if pulled by some invisible cord.

"I felt it," she said suddenly, her voice fuller now. "I felt it when I walked in... I didn't know why. But I felt something—strong. Familiar." Her gaze darted around, past the others, until it landed on me. "I'm Jackie," she said, her voice breaking ever so slightly. "I'm Jackie."

My hand loosened from the strap of Oscar's bag. My chest tightened, my breath shallow.

I wasn't sure if I was hearing her words or remembering them from a dream.

She stepped further into the room. *"Where is Benjamin?"*

It was like the name split the air open, dragging every piece of memory out from the back of my mind — the days in the dusty garden beds, her small hand cupping a sprouting, the last time we parted in that swirling wall of sand and noise. The things we never said.

Suddenly, Nana's words hit me with unshakable clarity. The Runes. The one she pressed into my palm when I was seven — Gebo, the symbol of a gift. *"Show me what I need to know about the future of Benjamin's life,"* she had whispered that night in the candlelight.

My pulse thundered. I turned slowly.

She saw me. I saw her.

And in that instant, everything between us collapsed — time, memory, distance. The child I once was stepped forward and handed me the moment. My feet moved before I could think.

I walked to her, disbelief still clinging to my movements. But my arms knew what to do. I wrapped them gently around her—like one might hold something precious found again after being lost for years.

She didn't hesitate.

She folded into the embrace like she had been waiting for it. Like her entire year abroad was meant to land her back here, at this exact doorstep, on this exact night.

No words passed between us. None were needed.

Whatever had started in Jerusalem was not finished.

Whatever Nana had seen, whatever the Runes had whispered—it was happening now.

And for the first time in years, I believed.

I t all came back to me—not in pieces, but in a rush, like floodwaters that had been waiting behind a gate that suddenly gave way.

I was still walking the line between being a boy and becoming something else. And on that day, Jerusalem had swallowed the light and left us standing in a wall of sand and silence.

We had been walking home from school, Jackie and I. The air that day was thick with wind, the sky a dull bronze. Sandstorms in that part of the world weren't new to us, but this one had come in faster than usual. It wasn't just dust—it carried something heavier, a kind of weight that seemed to settle on our skin, in our clothes, in our breath.

I still remember the way her braid whipped over her shoulder as we turned the corner. We were laughing — about something I can't even recall now — but the moment stopped cold when we reached my gate.

Mom stood outside, phone still in her hand, keys clenched tightly in the other. She received an urgent call from George Kuser telling her to grab what she could and to be at the airport within an hour. He stressed that it was imperative she told no one. Her eyes didn't blink. Her jaw was set. Her voice came quickly.

"Benjamin — come here."

There was no panic in her tone. That was what made it worse. There was no time for panic. Only urgency, sharp and cold.

I hesitated, confused. "What's going on?"

She opened the door without answering and disappeared inside.

I turned to Jackie, who hadn't said a word.

Her eyes had welled up, but she hadn't let a single tear fall. She was just staring at me. Staring like she already knew something I didn't.

"What's wrong?" I asked.

She looked down, then back up. Her voice was tight. "It's the sand again."

I glanced at the horizon, trying to convince myself it was just the weather making her like this. The sandstorm was picking up. Visibility was dropping. I chalked her mood up to that—to discomfort. I didn't think for a second that this would be the last time I'd see her.

Then, without warning, she grabbed my arm—not like a scared child, but like someone desperate to hold something still in a world that was shifting too fast. Her fingers pressed into my sleeve. She leaned in and hugged me with a force that caught me off guard. Then she pulled back—firm, steady.

"Goodbye," she whispered. Her voice didn't crack. "And God be with you."

That's when it hit me.

Something was wrong. Terribly wrong.

I tried to respond, but my mouth fumbled. "Everything will be okay," I said, trying to hold myself together. "Tomorrow, you'll see. We'll laugh about this. We'll—"

"Benjamin!" my mother's voice cut through again from inside the house.

I looked toward the door, then back to Jackie. I

couldn't move. I didn't want to. I didn't understand, but my body already knew—this moment wasn't going to be rewritten.

She handed me my books. Her fingers lingered on the edge of my hand. And then, without another word, she turned and started walking away, her figure swallowed slowly by the rising wind.

I stood there, my heart pounding, as the sand curled around my ankles and pulled at my coat.

Then I ran.

"Jackie!" I yelled, chasing after her voice, but the storm had already turned her into a shape in a blur. I waved wildly, my arms cutting the air, hoping she'd turn back—see me, know I hadn't wanted to go like this.

She never turned around.

Then, something shifted. I thought I saw her again, further away now, in a white robe, standing still against the backdrop of swirling sand. She didn't move. She didn't speak. Her arms were at her side. Her presence was calm, almost radiant, like some apparition pulled from one of Nana's old Rune readings.

I raised my hand again to wave, but my arm—froze midair. My chest filled with warmth, so suddenly that it stole my breath. A strange, comforting heat seemed to pour down my spine, spreading to my fingertips.

Then, just as fast, the wind returned, this time like a slap. The heat vanished. The chill hit me hard, ripping into my coat and eyes. I staggered backward, and my foot caught something—a step, a root—I couldn't tell.

Pain shot up my leg as I hit the ground, my chin smacking the dirt.

"Benjamin, get up!" my mother's voice again, close now. "We have to go! Are you okay?"

I tried to speak, but the air had gone. My lips moved, but it came out in a slur. "Yeah. I'm okay."

I felt her grab my arm, lifting me. My legs barely worked, but she kept pulling. We moved fast, my body half-dragging, half-running, back into the house.

And then—darkness.

When I woke, it was cold.

Not outside cold, but sterile cold—the kind that lives in metal and glass. There was a weight on my forehead, something damp. I turned my head instinctively, and the cold pad slipped to the floor.

My eyes adjusted slowly to the narrow light above me. My ears were plugged, filled with a pressure that made the world muffled and far away. I blinked hard and looked out the nearest window—small, oval, fogged slightly around the edges.

I was on a plane.

My chest seized.

My mind raced to catch up. My hand clutched at the armrest, my knuckles white. I pressed my face to the window, trying to see through the blur, and for a moment—I swear—I saw Jerusalem below. I saw the rooftops, the lines of the city streets, the homes I had walked past every day. It was slipping out of view.

I opened my mouth, and wanted to call out her name. I wanted to rewind the last hour, to go back, to run harder. But no words came.

Just tears.

Then, over the hum of the cabin, a soft whisper near my ear.

"Everything is okay, son," my mother said. *"We're going home. To America."*

*"If one advances
confidently in the
direction of his dreams,
and endeavors to live the
life which he has
imagined, he will meet
with a success unexpected
in common hours.
He will put some things
behind, will pass an
invisible boundary; new,
universal, and more
liberal laws will begin to
establish themselves
around and within him;
or the old laws be
expanded, and
interpreted in his favor in
a more liberal sense, and
he will live with the
license of a higher order
of beings."*

Henry David Thoreau

Where I Lived, and What I Lived For from the book Walden (1854)

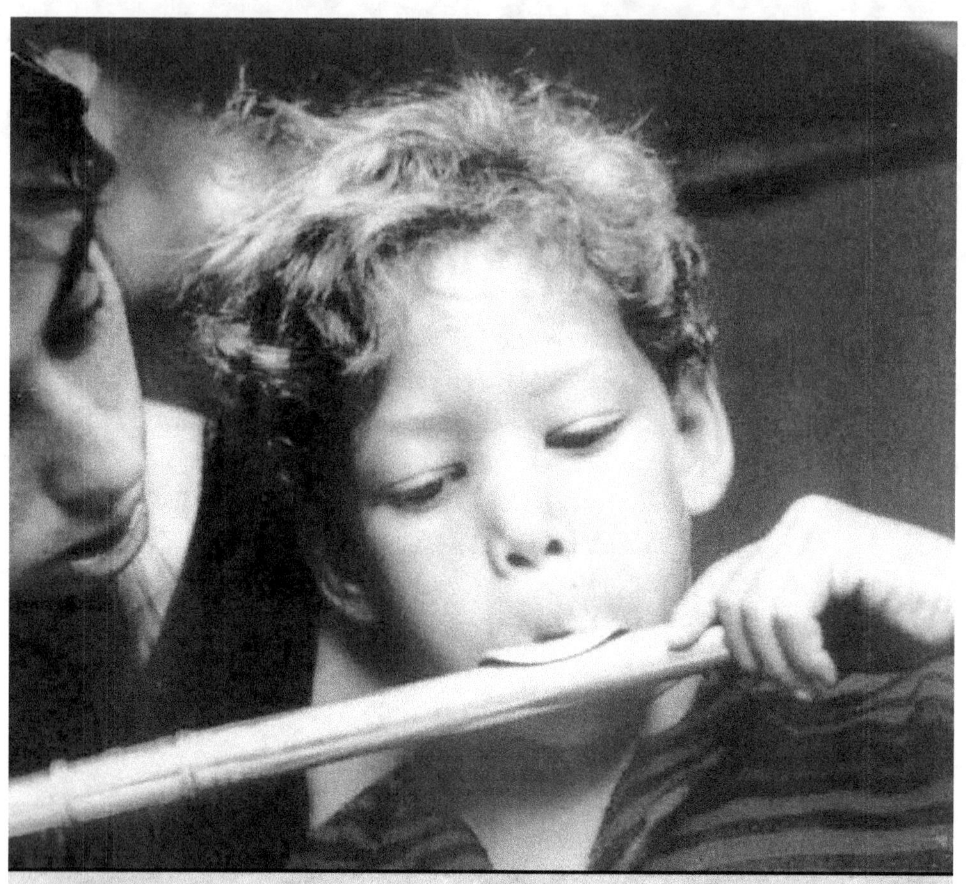

"The Music Lesson"

Epilogue

As it was in the beginning, the future paths one travels during their life stages are not solely determined by time or place alone, but through the foresightedness of others who have made the journey before us, who were also showered with the profoundness of a forever caregiver's love; they also inherit and possess the wisdom that paints the portrait of destiny.

Benjamin's grandmother, Marganita "Maggie" Cohen-Grabowsky's window to the world goes beyond the roll of the Gift Rune. She has heard the visions of the crimes against humanity from her parents, which shielded her youth from the unexpected in a plan.

However that young love mixed with no fear became the 'rose color' strength, a courageous blindness to make the journey; leaving her homeland, although supposedly temporary, she packed the 'seed' – the one that Ralph Waldo Emerson spoke of: *"Though we travel the world over to find the beautiful, we must carry it with us or we find it not."*

After Maggie and Asa left St. Petersburg on *Freedom's Destiny,* so many life-altering events happened which are now revealed in this new 2025 novel version of the *Wisdom of Nana via Gebo Passage.* The lives of the Grabowsky-Cohan-Cohen families as well as the others were not only filled with heartwarming and smooth sailing jubilations, but also heart-wrenching tragedies.

Although packaged as fiction, the **Wisdom of Nana via the Gebo Passage** does not actually embellish or disguise in entirety the realities of the lives of others interwoven into this read about family, faith, cultural heritage and career paths. Probably best said by author

Marge Kennedy, *"Soup is a lot like a family. Each ingredient enhances the others; each batch has its own characteristics; and it needs time to simmer to reach full flavor."*

The future lives of the Grabowsky-Cohan-Cohen-Smith ancestral bloodline: Nathan, Sarah, Benjamin, Jackie, cousins, aunts, uncles, French foster child Ginny, Tirone, Elizabeth, Derrick are yet to be told as they embark upon scores of social, political, economics, and technological changes that will connect them closer, whether with a friend of a friend, even those associations made during their bread 'n butter careers as well as not limited to the present unknown generations and those to come in America and abroad.

In the forthcoming sequel, the reunion between Benjamin and Jackie, now sealed by fate, was the very partnership his grandmother had predicted—a bond that would carry their family into new generations, a union blessed by the wisdom of the past. The love between them would plant seeds of hope for the future, growing into a legacy that would outlast even the shadows that sought to destroy them.

For in the choices they made and in the magic that flowed through their veins, the past, present, and future were forever intertwined. And with Jackie by his side, the story of their family would continue to unfold—through generations yet to come, and through the memories of those who had already passed. ♥

Wonderness of Youse

Ben Rayman

"Night Walk"

Portraits of Life

My Seductress Southern Belle

My Fearless Bro-by-Law

Head West Young Lass

Your Deal

"Samantha Jo"

My Seductress Southern Belle

"Animals are such agreeable friends - they ask no questions, they pass no criticisms."

George Eliot

The first time I ever saw her face, it was a gleaming bright sunny morning. The ground had been blanketed with a new fresh snow during the night. As I sat in the bay window of the kitchen clad only in my pajama bottom, cradling a hot steamy cup of coffee in my palms, the lenses of my eye glasses fogged up with every sip. I could tell the outdoors was frigid. I could feel the snow's crispness as it glistened with an ice-like hardness. I had to put on my robe until the heat took the chill off the room. Minutes later, my body was feeling regret because my mind did not want to surrender the warmness. However, I knew I had to get ready for work and brave the assault of the external coldness.

As I swung open the back door porch door, the wind slapped me in the face. I felt my facial skin tighten. I purged my lungs with the morning air and began to slowly pan my farthest surroundings. The outdoors gave me the feeling of purity; however that quickly changed as I stood over an open hole on the porch floor. The freezing air gushed up my slacks and I felt the goose pumps on my thighs. Simultaneously, I recall wishing I had put on my long johns when I spotted her eagerly approaching me in a cunning way.

My immediate thoughts registered an *Oh No!* I was already behind schedule and I didn't have the time to get involved. I wanted to push this misfortune animal away from me, but I could not muster up that manlike trait needed to forget about another life and to remain emotionless because I was faced with this situation twice before. I knew the domestic cat population was in the mega millions in the United States, but I could not bring myself to make an abrupt exit because only half belonged to homes. Furthermore, money was not a deterrent and another mouth to feed would not jeopardize our family financial framework.

She had a meticulous southern-like charming style; I figured she was sort of an Artisan in the game of mating. Her passionate pleas grabbed at my heartstrings. My vision doubled and then teardrops started to stream from my face.

Her scrawny frame was enhanced only by her haggard eyes, but her voice hummed feelings of love. It was obvious she was not getting the right amount of sleep and the ever-increasing intermittent rumbles from her abdomen were not signs of gas, but pains-of-hunger. She hovered around me like an airplane waiting to land. She weaved in and out brushing lightly up against my body. Through her thin-ragged overcoat, the touch of her softness made my heart tremble.

I asked her what she was doing out in this brutal weather, but she did not respond. I told her to go home, but she said nothing. Then suddenly, swirling arctic wind made me rush to the garage to take cover. I summoned her to come in and she blurted out a lonely screeching cry. I attempted to comfort her by brushing her hair away from her face and told her I would return.

As I headed back into my house, I could see her peering out of the garage door window. I felt her anticipation for food, and when I returned, she was turning in circles. She devoured the toss-together meal as if it was her last. Hurriedly, I went back into the house for more food. As she ate, I went and laid a blanket on the patio lounge. I told her she was welcome to stay until she is ready to go home. Soon after, I left for work.

On my way home, I began to feel a great deal of empathy for the homeless female. I couldn't get her impoverished appearance out of my mind. I kept wondering if she had made her way back to her family. Even though, I know charity starts at home, I knew from firsthand experience the reality of being used. I just didn't want to have to endure a past of jumble of events. I knew they would conjure up deep-rooted hurt feelings from sticking my neck out helping others. I have been burned too many times and I often thought if sucker was written on my forehead in indelible ink. Nevertheless, I hoped she would still be there, nestled in the heavy blanket I left so I could finish my Good Samaritan deed.

About four blocks from home, I prepared myself for the possibility that I would not be able to finish my goodhearted goal. I calmed my zealous confidence using the old counting to ten theory. It was working because I kept thinking how supportive the girls, Daisy Mae and Mindy Lou would be. They would humbly accept the possibility of a new baby sister.

The car radio was tuned to Fort Wayne's Magic 95.1. They were playing the oldies from my teen years. I heard the faint music of The Captain and Tennille. They were singing, *Love Will Keep Us Together*. The song's words were doing a tug-of-war number with my emotions. I thought of switching the music to rock. With the volume at an ear-piercing loudness, it would force a hard-heartedness. It worked and I felt prepared for anything.

Entering the driveway, I pushed the remote control to open the door. I drove in and shut down the engine. I sat a few minutes in the quiet starring stiffly forward. My mind kept repeating a line from that oldie song, "You belong to me now." I turned the key on so the radio would make music to forestall the negative presupposition she is gone struggle.

Nonchalantly, I started to look for her; saw nothing. Presumed gone. I swung open my door and like a shooting star, she jumped up on my lap --- brushing and turning ---

her head against my chest; purring those feelings of love. Gleefully, I caressed my seductress southern belle in my arms and crowned her Samantha Jo. She climbed higher up around my neck and I smoothed my cheeks over her soft fur. Instantly, my mind recognized the music playing. The singer sung the line describing what I was feeling and I whispered to her those words: *The Lion Sleeps Tonight*.

I am happy to report; Sammie Jo filled my life with thirteen years of happiness. ♥

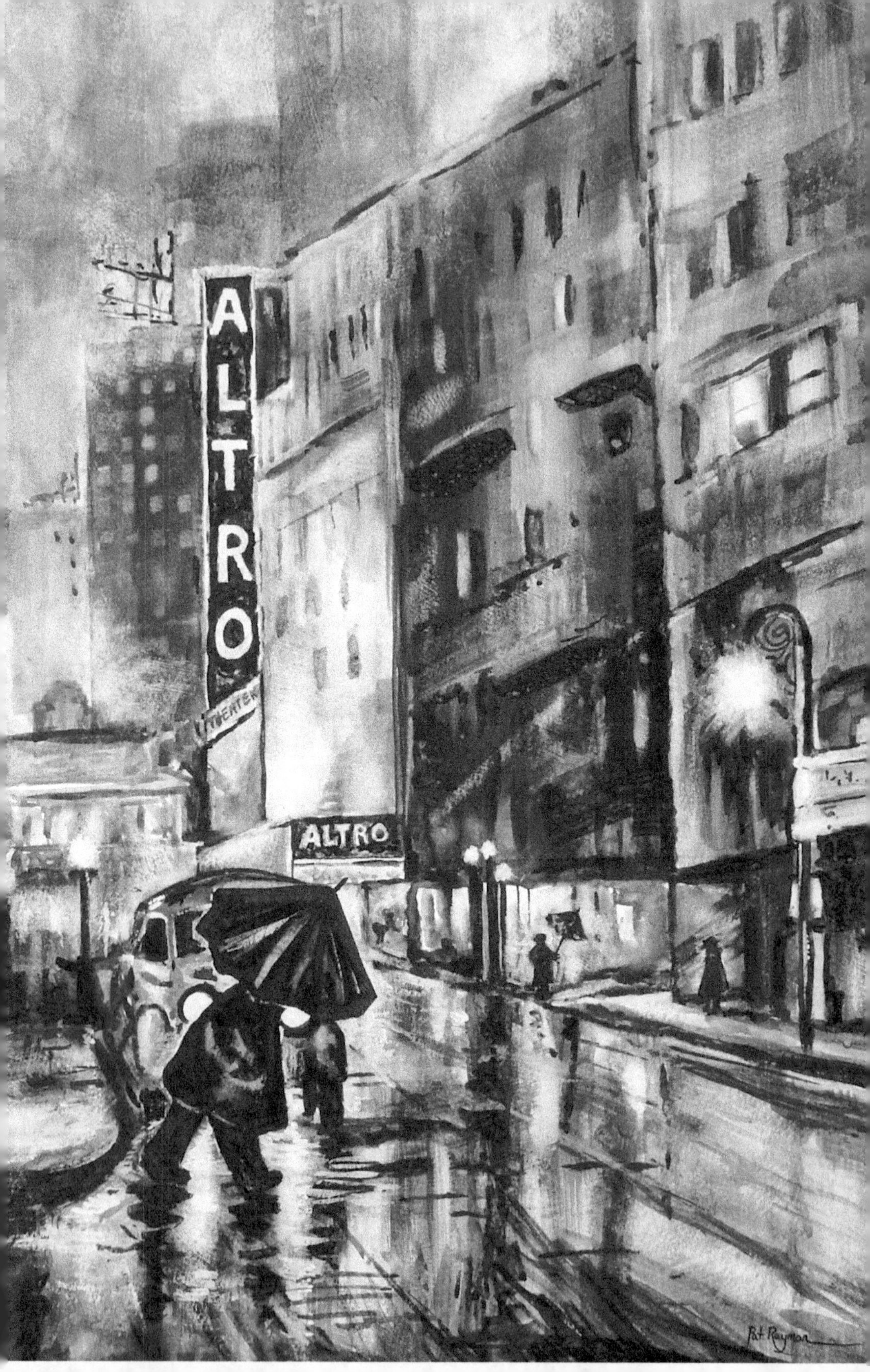

ALTRO
THEATER
ALTRO
Pat Rayman

My Fearless Bro-by-Law

The first time I met the eldest, Roody, his omniscient talents intrigued me. Although he has spent most of his career in the communication industry at New Jersey Bell, I believe he missed his calling as an entertainer. Whether it's tinkling the ivories, slinging drinks, creating his voluminous gourmet cuisine known as *'The Roody Burger'* on the outdoor grill, or serving not only as the tour guide but also the chauffeur when we all piled into his *'New York City limo'* — the bottom line is I never left his domain with wishful recollections.

For those who do not know what a 'New York City limo' is, let me paint a picture in terms of era and geography. It is one of those classic luxury liners that emerged from the 1950s. You can sit behind the wheel and almost need binoculars to gauge the distance between you and the car in front of you! Come to think of it, I can recall seeing Roody's car in a rerun of an A-Team episode. I thought the vehicle was out of place, but then I later understood that a German tank wasn't at their disposal. I often wondered if those Freedom Fighters were Roody's idols because of their successful abilities to improvise; moreover, his addictive loyalty to the tube when Hannibal and his merry global wanderers were beckoned to serve those in need. Nevertheless, it all became clear to me later: *"If you are going into the city, if it looks like the south end of a horse going north, stay away,"* fervently emphasized Roody.

Sooner than I anticipated, we embarked upon the royal tour. As Roody's arm encircled my neck, he exclaimed, *"It is time to introduce this Buckeye to the city that never sleeps!"* Then he politely invited my mate, *"It is time to board."* Finally, he appealed to his other half, *"Get the lead out — we are going slumming!"*

From the Jersey side, we crossed over the George Washington Bridge. As we motored further into Bronx territory, my sister-in-law tossed out, in her signature style of recall tone, *"Look, Patty! Over there is the zoo. Remember when Mommy and Daddy used to take us there?"*

Roody quipped, *"Yeah, Pat, that's where I met Barb!"* Suddenly, I saw a flash of an arm, and then Roody let out a chuckling groan. I must have been sporting a mischievous grin, and as I turned to my wife, she said in her authoritarian way, *"Don't you start!"* Laughter then filled the air.

As we traveled the expressway, Roody made a

speedy swoop over the Whitestone Bridge into the Flushing area. I learned later that he was giving the sisters a memory lane jaunt.

As young girls, they would visit their mother's mother, and I knew Pat held no childhood joy of her grandmother. I broke the emotional silence with a question, inquiring if the airport was nearby. This successfully triggered Roody to head southeast to JFK International. Eventually, we ended up driving past Coney Island, which got all the non-New Yorkers talking about their joyful memories. Then, our host driver made a northern upshot all the way into Manhattan.

Oddly, I felt like we were just taking a leisurely Sunday drive in the country. There were no delays, and we got lots of sightseeing from Roody's backstage auditorium. However, that changed as we toured through Chinatown.

We got caught in the city bus runs. Instead of Roody staying to his left as the road widened, the 'limo' found itself vertical with the bus. Traffic was as deep as an anthill, and it became a slow inch-by-inch process for Roody to work the 'limo' into the main lane.

"Ben, you're in New York City now! Watch this guy try to shove his way in front of us," Roody said, chomping and rolling his smokeless cigar.

Well, I did! But Fearless Roody kept nudging the front passenger fender of the 'hogmobile' against the rear of the bus. His goal was to not let his left competitor squeeze even a millimeter from the space needed to pass first.

"Sorry, Joe, I'm not giving," muttered our ship's captain. Fortunately, only the wing of Roody's New York City 'Titanic' was bruised as it navigated its way through both sides of its opponents.

With this being my first exposure to life in the fast lane, I later understood why you wouldn't stop to engage in a self-investigation of a New York City summit of fenders:

First, you would have to get out of your car, which would be almost a superhuman feat involving snaking your way through a window.

Second, it would provoke an avalanche of car horns blaring nonstop. Of course, they wouldn't be tooting their approval like a wedding procession. Somehow, I felt fortunate not to be able to read lips as heads protruded from car windows.

Third, imagine trying to explain how your rendezvous happened in a calm tone while standing next to a busload of passengers who had to be at their destination yesterday. And, of all things, to a driver who spoke a universal language that you know well but doesn't belong to a specific country.

Meanwhile, as we proceeded onward from the aftermath of the earlier thrill, Barbara decided the new objective was to find a place to park near Fifth Avenue. *"It's time to shop till we drop,"* the matriarch echoed with great anticipation.

Pat had already prepared me for the fact that her sister inherited that shopping gene from their mother. She warned me there weren't any Bonanza Steakhouses in the city. I determined, only after the fact that she was trying to tell me not to order the salad.

Somehow, I must have resented her advice.

Somehow, I should have seriously considered her twenty-five-dollar estimation as gospel because back in Ohio, I could have gotten a full-course meal for less than ten.

Somehow, I can only surmise that my miscalculation of the cost for an egg, a tomato, and green leaves tossed on a plate was a peak of foolishness during my early twenties.

Nevertheless, I have to say it ranks right up there with that male mental blockade of not stopping to ask for directions when lost.

With my Ohio genealogical roots firmly bound in Putnam County—Farmland, USA—I have a clear-cut definition of what is sublime and what is ridiculous. It never dawned on me that an empty parking space would command the same hourly wage as a Ford Motor factory worker! Additionally, my mind wasn't calculating the length of a New York City block based on  football field measurements. Nor did I perceive that I would have to walk at a jog pace and view the sights panoramically.

Despite the fact that my current marital status was still in that honeymoon year, I soon thought to myself that I didn't have to worry about my wallet flying away because I relocated it to my front pants pocket. Fortunately, with no second thoughts, I did not resist this suggestion from Pat.

On the other hand, for those with an imagination, window shopping through a certain portion of 42nd Street afforded me a fascinating sensation. Under the presumption that the euphoria I felt was due to my innocence, I became awestruck by the scenic artwork.

My stride suddenly slowed to a turtle pace as the trio forged ahead. I kept moving my head and eyes as if I were playing Pac-Man. I was dumbfounded by all that I was seeing and subliminally hearing. I just couldn't believe this was so open to the general public.

In retrospect, as I wandered aimlessly, I must have been mistaken for one of the locals. With my jaw almost to the ground and that spinning sensation you get after being turned in circles before you attempt to pin the donkey's tail, I must have muted an invitation.

I discovered the giver was not someone I had said "I do" to earlier that year. Though my gold band was not obvious, which earmarked my chosen union, I must assume he was definitely nearsighted because my hippie insignia was in my straight ear.

Unfortunately, the sensation was near the area where I kept my American Express checks; however, he assured me through hands-on experience that I didn't leave home without them!

In those memory lane flashbacks, I am certain my evaluation of Roody's missed career path can only be

Photo by Angelo Rizzuto

captured in a quote by Robert Kirby of the Utah County Journal: *"The mark of a true professional is giving more than you get."* Since Mr. Kirby does not know Roody, I must also affirm that New York City can be referred to as 'the place'—a virtual potpourri of the sublime and the ridiculous.

However, I have discovered that it is a city blessed. The metropolis is embedded with an international richness of many cultures, enhanced by the performing and visual arts alongside architecture that reaches for the clouds, solidifying its status as a world-class emporium for commerce. New York City truly balances the scale between indifference and admiration, possessing it all while at the same time stirring a rage of discomfort with its external human suffering. But, those opinions deserve respect because it has always welcomed all who enter, regardless of their means.

On our way home that night, I recall turning back and seeing the city aglow from the Garden State side. The lights resembled a conflagration, which filled me with warmth and overshadowed my fears from the day's

events. The reason for this was Roody's courage; it was contagious. I knew I would return because I had amassed a vast collection of joyful memories. ♥

"Down along in the Shenango River Valley"

Head West Young Lass

When Horace Greeley (1811-72) advocated the migration to the west, chances are he never had women in mind when he popularized the phrase "Go West, young man." However, a century after his passing, **Patricia (Grabowski) Rayman** discovered the reality of her childhood avocation as she tells, *"I would look out my bedroom window and somehow I sensed I was being drawn westward."*

Born in New Jersey of Polish-Russian ancestry during the start of the baby-boomer generation, Pat is a roundly pleasing petite woman who stands a shade over five feet tall with blonde streaks running through her semi-short brunette hair. With a humble personality that illuminates, she subliminally bridles those who only distinguish others by appearance, social, economic or knowledge statuses, consequently challenging the discriminatory minds to search within themselves to see those true inner beauty qualities of all human beings.

Initially educated by professional artists from New York City, and later completing her degree in education from Baltimore's *Maryland Institute of Art*, Pat declined career opportunities to apply her creative skill as an illustrator for an eminent greeting card company on New York's Madison Avenue as well as to remain and teach art education within her roots.

After a summer teaching post ended where she worked with special children, she ventured to Delphos, a rural agricultural city located in the Northwestern central corridor of Ohio, and has taught elementary and middle school children for over 32 years for the public schools. However, her teaching is not limited to children, yet continues to teach art workshops locally and out-of-state.

Patricia Rayman not only practices what she teaches, but has realized years later, *"Those first two years in art school — and being taught by professionals — made the transition to education a success for me and for my children."* For me, the why is no longer a wonder, but a pride because she has been showered with hundreds of awards for her own art and photography.

Concurrently over the years, she has been selected as *Big Sister of the Year* for her involvement in a

young girl's life which allowed this child to bud from a thorny environment and blossom forward with noted local and national achievements. She was also selected *Tri-County Woman-of-the-Year* for her volunteerism and an undaunted willingness of providing encouragement: Art is ageless, not only to the young, but even among nursing home seniors.

Pat has been recognized by the *Ohio Senate* for her humanitarian contributions which goes back to her younger years working with emotionally and physically handicapped children. In addition, she also received an *Outstanding Achievement in Education* award as the founder of **Art-to-Art: Building Friendships Through Art**, a national art-based education program which bridges the gap with the subjects of Geography, History, Reading, Writing, and Communications through Human Relations. Her so-far life's travels reads like a Who's Who list; in fact, she was included in *Who's Who In America* in the past.

When I met Pat, it was late spring of 1974. The country was in an economic upheaval with interests rates rising to levels untouched in the recorded past, inflation continuing its rapid increase, unemployment rising and The House Judiciary Watergate Committee was formally notifying President Richard Nixon that his defiance of subpoenas might constitute a ground for impeachment which lead to his resignation in August. Although I was working in the newspaper industry, none of these events worried me because she captured the heart, mind, and soul of a young man in search of a life partner.

To this day, I still cannot understand the astrophysical reason for her journey West, some 700 miles away from her roots, with no immediate family or friends because I know Pat would have realized Frank Sinatra's sung words to the hilt and *"...made it in New York,"* nevertheless I have seized that inner mental reservation by the plainly put words of St. Paul: *"We walk by faith, not by sight."* She has provided me with the freedom to explore those less traveled roads where others could only savor; I could feast upon an affluence of real world knowledge gained from my own belief that life's real voyage of discovery consists not in seeking new landscapes, but in having new eyes, and through her eyes, I saw my ability to embrace adversities, to envision possibilities while traveling among the skeptics, and soaring through the undergrowths others would pass by.

And finally, each day becomes more vivid as I recall a line from one of Lou Rawls' songs: *"You'll never meet a love like mine as long as you live,"* and I can only exclaim: ***Yawantabet!!*** ♥

"Winter's Makeup"

Your Deal . . .

I t came every year, a tradition that involved two men. Their lives transformed during their annual family gatherings. What I had thought card playing was all about—a friendly game of socialization—I came to learn was a set of flat pieces of thin cardboard, ornamented with figures and numbers, usually rectangular in shape with rounded edges, which were my brother-in-law's weapon in a bloodless war of skill.

In 1975, Bob entered my life when I became the youngest "recruit" in the Grabowsky family through my marriage to Pat, his wife's sister. It never crossed my mind that someday, it would become a struggle to say goodbye to him while holding onto the same happiness that had once filled me with anticipation and sustained me during those long dawn-to-dusk 800-mile trips from Indiana to New York.

During our first round of two weeks of seasonal togetherness, Bob and I spent countless hours in activities that left us caught between youth and adulthood. They brought out not only the sublime but also the ridiculous in us both. Spring was our time to create new beginnings, keeping the relationship fresh.

We were separated in age by a generation and a half, yet our likeness in things, lifestyle, and ideals felt unique. I was more open-minded and liberal in thought; however, I was always dumbfounded by how he expressed what I was thinking. Frankly, he gave my thoughts verbal life, and they usually surfaced when I was driving in his war zone. Sometimes our communications were almost telepathic.

"That broad must have gotten her license at K-Mart!" Bob cheered.

I smiled and raised my hand, as if to ask her to choose a finger. He followed with one of his favorite quotations: *"Craft must have clothes, but truth loves to go naked."* As I weaved around her, he sat motionless, staring ahead, and gave her the salute. Once past, our pent-up laughter burst out simultaneously.

We never seemed to run out of conversation, regardless of the topic; the same went for Pat and Bob's wife, Janet. The sisters, whom we sometimes forgot were riding in the back seat with us, created their own world. But eventually, certain comments would join us all in conversation.

"I can't wait to see the Met," Pat said excitedly.

I looked at Bob and voiced to him nervously, "I'd need to spend a couple more weeks in this area first to gear myself up for people and cars coming out of my posterior—day and night."

Bob chuckled and, in a nasally tone, said, *"Wait until we get into the city. Just don't bend over."*

He knew about my first indoctrination to New York's 42nd Street with Rudy and Barbara, the eldest in-laws. I saluted him for his wisdom and expressed my gratitude for the reminder of that hands-on experience.

Each year, like clockwork, the Monday before Memorial Day at 4:00 AM, Pat and I left our Nashville, Indiana home and would arrive at Bob's right after the sun had set on the East Coast.

I found it to be quite an adventure to Bob's house once off the New York State Thruway. Similar to how Little Miss Riding Hood had traveled to her grandma's, I exited the interstate at Albany/Schenectady, where it intersects with I-88 heading to Binghamton. I had to go through a section built during the late 40s. It smelled of old money.

As I made my first turn onto St. Sebastian Lane, it became an endless series of twists and turns, up and down hilly terrain, with large oak and elm trees lining both sides of the road for a good five miles.

I couldn't help wondering who lived in those massive three- and four-story homes of brick and mortar. I always thought those homes would make a New York City brownstone appear small. They sat back off the road, over 300 feet, surrounded by towering trees and evergreens of various colors. The late afternoon sun streamed down through the treetops, striking the huge French windows with endless shades of light. Those scenes reminded me of artworks by Thomas Kinkade, the painter of light.

Bob lived in a new housing addition built in the 80s, developed for young executive families, mainly the offspring of those who lived off St. Sebastian. A ditch separated the two developments, draining excess water into the Mohawk River.

Bob always said, *"We live in the servant's section."* It was his way of letting others know he was just a regular middle-class Joe, even though his home was statuesque.

Regardless of the time—day or night—I always knew where to turn because the road began a steep descent into a long angling S-curve that swerved to the left, then right. At the bottom, I crossed a covered bridge, and then Bob's house was on Cherry Blossom Drive. Located at the end of a cul-de-sac and situated in the center of the circle's arc, there were no houses on either side because it was considered an odd size—231 feet wide and 77 feet deep.

The road had many of those old oaks and elms on both sides; it mirrored the same hilly landscape as the old-money section, narrow as an inner-city neighborhood side street for a good mile.

The road wound and dipped to the right, making me think of a cartoon thought bubble in a cloud shape. Within a short distance, as the road started to turn left, everything opened again. It made me think of the scene where Julie Andrews is twirling around while singing in The Sound of Music on the mountaintop.

Bob later told me this was where farmers would rest and water their oxen. This explained the only aged old trees in Forest Park and the wishing well in the middle of the cul-de-sac. For historical reasons, the developers left the old well and landscaped around it.

His house is one of the first in this raised ranch-style section. However, Bob's home is like him — private. It is shaped like an oversized stretch limousine, 120 feet long and 40 feet wide, constructed at the top of the lot's crest. The half-circle driveway entrance was carved into road level, leading to and arcing under a two-story covered front entrance. From the road, you can only see a car's side windows.

Pulling in the drive, I could see Bob swaying back and forth in front of the large picture window. I knew how the living room furniture was arranged. His favorite rocking chair was to the far left, giving him a full view of those coming and going. It also allowed him a view of his masonry handiwork, a six-foot-high, 200-foot long retaining wall. Bob was in his usual kneeling position with his arms propped up and his hands underneath his chin, reminding me of a kid waiting for his dad to come home.

What always surprised me was not his 5'6" height, but his youthful looks. He had no facial sags or lines. His job as a scientific research technological engineer never affected his eyes to the point that he needed glasses. There was not a stitch of gray or baldness in his jet-black hair—not bad for a man in his mid-50s. I would always ask him what his secret was.

"It's called a Manhattan, and plenty of them," he quipped. I guess I never saw the signs, although I was knowledgeable enough about what alcohol does to the human body's internal organs.

After the first night's dinner, it was always a given that the Wednesday before and the Wednesday after Decoration Day would be spent at the lake house in the Adirondack Mountains. This was the time when the old cliché, "absence makes the heart grow fonder," rang true; our renewed friendship thrived with daily contact. It also marked the beginning of a new round of seasonal reunions for the four of us, with the opening of the summer house.

Bob and I did the outdoor tasks: putting the boat dock in the water, cranking down all the window awnings that gave this elephant of a house a different character, setting up the outdoor furniture, and firing up the grill for our first lunchtime down by the water. Pat and Janet took care of the inside.

Bob called it *"the camp,"* which was built in the 30s. The house felt like a year-round home. It was a two-and-a-half-story, six-bedroom, three-and-a-half-bathroom place with room-to-room fireplaces, huge screened-in porches on every side, and complete with separate servant quarters. I always thought, if this was a camp, what a way to rough it.

"New York Flower Shop"

Bob was diagnosed with a terminal illness. In retrospect, I understood how he extended his life almost three years beyond the initial six months given. It wasn't just the unconditional care from his wife of over 30 years or the deep-rooted love he had for her; it was also the pride he felt for his sons, Johnny and Bobby, who grew into solid young men. Toward the end, it became increasingly difficult for me to muster the strength to say goodbye to my best friend and soldier-in-marriage.

Like most reunions, the fun never began until past life events were hashed over during dinner. Our first set of warm-up card games was launched after the main course while we waited for dessert to be served by the living room fireplace.

Dirty Harry was the card game of choice. I would always win the first round because he had cooled off since Christmas. However, as the games proceeded, I used to wonder if he had his deck of cards rigged. His eyebrows would rapidly flutter up and down like Groucho Marx's, and I could see his eyes fill with a happy glassiness. Bob always ended up with the 2s, 4s, and Queens when I dealt.

From years of experience, I knew I had it coming; yet I kept a poker face and hit him with all I had to forestall the inevitable.

"It's in ALLLL how they fall," he repeated.

Then, it was his turn. In a monotone voice, Bob would say, *"Pick up two, pick up two, back to me, and skip your turn. Your deal!"*

I muttered my dissatisfaction, and then he let out, *"LOVEEE this game!"*

Fortunately, the old cliché "what goes around comes around" proved to be a winning theory for me. I pulled out my lucky deck. I changed my strategy, held all my wild cards, and let him dump on me first. Just when he was in that manic high, I would let him have it: *"Pick up two, skip your turn, pick up two, back to me,"* and orally heightened the tension by chanting *"uno, uno, uno,"* signifying that I would be going out next.

"You don't got it!" he bellowed.

Most of the time, I didn't have the matching card and had to draw, but usually hit a card I could lay down. To keep the mental havoc alive, I would keep unoing him because he had a handful of cards. This became our nightly event. We played for hours, forgetting *"who dealt that last mess!"* which was Bob's usual remark, as he attempted to focus on the surroundings instead of the coffee table.

These times always reminded me of what Henry Thoreau said: "To be active, well, happy implies rare courage. To be ready to fight in a duel implies desperation, or that you hold your life cheap." I believed the poet's underlying message — that routine is a ground to stand on, and surely joy is a condition of life.

At the end of our time together, Bob gleamed with a restored optimistic outlook for the future. They would be coming to Indiana. We talked about what we would do during the annual Autumn Festival in Brown County. Although the four of us would spend quality time together, we would eventually split, with Jane and Pat going to the art galleries and museums, while Bob and I would head to my houseboat docked on Yellowwood Lake.

We spent the whole day cruising in and out of the lake's 133-acre primitive inlets and anchored to fish for a while at each remote stop. Then we'd make our way to McCabe's, a one-room rustic bar and grill. Inside and out, this hideaway glowed with color lights. From top to bottom, the walls were lined with all types of beer signs and a few dartboards. A pool table, three pinball machines, and several card tables filled the room.

This was our favorite off-the-beaten-path retreat because all the male customers were at the height of slob fashion, and Chef Herbie made a hamburger that would make the average greasy spoon jealous — not to mention the many drinks required to wash it down during our card games.

I n September 1994, Bob didn't make it to Indiana. I went to New York instead. I asked him to hold onto my deck of cards. They were a birthday gift from him. On each card was inscribed a quote by French novelist Colette: *"By means of an image we are often able to hold onto our lost belongings. But it is the desperateness of losing that picks the flowers of memory, binds the bouquet."* ♥

Attributions

Works of Watercolors, Acrylics, Pen and Inks, Photography by Patricia Rayman

Dawn Fog (p6); Windy Point (p10); A Beacon to Freedom (p12);

Delphos Elevator (p20); A Light in the Forest (p28); A Brand New Day (p46);

The Windy Winter (p73); Irish Cottage by the Lake, (p80);

Hoosier Highway (p85);Waldoboro, ME Market (p100);

Blessing from Above (p104); Vision's Whispers (p120);

A Long Way Home (p122); Nordman Lake Haven (p148); Tall Timbers (p178);

Albert Einstein (p192); Drying Times on the Farm (p213);

Maria von Trapp (p216); Aging Beauty (p234); Home Again (p252);

Music Lesson (p270); Nightwalk (p274); Samantha Jo (p276, 282);

Altro (p282); Down along in the Shenango River Valley (p292);

Winter's Makeup (p297); A Quiet Night (p317)

Other pictorials

Destiny, AAPB, (p173)

World Map, Maps of the World © 2013 (174-175)

Destinations, AAPB (176)

Magic Box of Tales & Truths , Wisdom Collection Series, (p318)

Poetry and other literary works

The Road Not Taken, (p11) Robert Frost {3-26-1874-01-29-1963}

A Heart's Icon (p252); Ben Rayman

Where I Live, and What I Lived For, from the book *Walden* (1854) (p269)
Henry David Thoreau {7-12-1817-5-6-1862}

Wonderness of Youse (p273) Ben Rayman

Wisdom of Nana via Gebo Passage

CAST OF CHARACTERS

Marganita Cohen-Grabowsky
Benjamin Grabowsky
Peter Solomon Cohen
Rebecca Greenbaum-Cohen
Asa Grabowsky
Nathan Grabowsky
Sarah Cohan-Grabowsky
Ginny Brinkman
Thomas Brinkman
Sara Morgret-Brinkman
Asher Grabowsky
Rachel Fischer-Grabowsky
Charlotte Grabowsky
Abigail Grabowsky
Sarah Grabowsky
Billy Atenwood,
Oscar Stone
Esther Fogt-Stone
Joyce Marie Stone
Carol Ann Stone
Edward Coleman
Victoria Coleman
Jackie Coleman
Bobby Coleman
Edward Smith
Elizabeth Moreau-Smith
Pierre Moreau
Mary Louise Durand
Bernard Dubois
Jacques Dubois
Catherine Bonnet-Dubois
Tirone Smith, Ship's captain
Ellis, Ship's cook
Henrik, Ship Helmsman
Jakob, Ship's carpenter
Dutch, British, Scandinavian sailors
Levi Bernard

Abigail Goldberg-Bernard
Asher Samuel Bernard
Joanne Wieman
Murray Bernard
Virginia Bernard
Roberta Bernard
Jennifer Bernard
Barbara Bernard
Principal Sommers
Esther Bierman
Reporter Simmons
Ruth Ann Dunkin
Philip Goldstein
Al McPherson
George Kuser
Edward Welch
Cousin Jeff Jones
Uncle Johnny Fogt
Aunt Jeanie Carter-Fogt
Derrick Hatcher
Samantha McLaughlin-Hatcher
Maude Carson
Kimberly Byrne
Carter Dupont
Ava Freedman-Dupont
Josephine "Josie" Dupont
Johnny Johnson
David Price
Louis Dubois
Peter Dubois
Frederick Johnson
Gregory Anthony Byrne-Smith
Monique Susan Dupont-Smith
And a cast of many others as
Freedom's Destiny and *Prince of Tide*
travels the Globe.

Abouts

Ben Rayman's writing, both in fiction and non-fiction, captures the essence of realism with a unique touch. He highlights the individuals involved in significant events, weaving their stories together with a kind and thoughtful wit. His style is approachable and relatable, creating a gentle yet profound connection with readers.

He is the founder and serves in an Editor's capacity for the *Art-to-Art Palette Journal*, a U.S. national publication that is produced in print as well as digitally in a different editorial forum, serving the Arts and Educational communities.

Founded in 1986, the *Art-to-Art Palette Journal* (AAPJ) began publishing and established its central objective: "*. . . to serve as a contributing media for the promotion and support of the arts, an advocate for continued education and for the organizations, groups, societies, clubs and creative minds throughout the United States including beyond its borders.*"

The *Palette* has mainly published in print with an editorial content that records the histories, featuring artists, educators and the entities, including extensive readings of related topics. AAPJ graphically takes on a magazine design, but printed on a heavier glossy paper stock for preservation purposes.

"Editorially, it is not a magazine. I would classify the *Palette* to hover in the middle between a trade journal that serves a specific industry, profession, trade or business," said Rayman. The *Palette* not only contains much educational content from history to how-to-do-it, but it also reports on all art forms. The publication has also been labeled a Who's Who journal as it individually shines the spotlight directly on artists, educators, and entities for their gifts and achievements.

AAPJ began in service as the national spokesmedia for the *Art-to-Art: Building Friendships Through Art* (1986-2006), an Ohio-based k-12 national art education program. "The Art-to-Art program is a complete another About and could easily produced enough content to be published in a dozen or so books," said Rayman.

However, he explained to understand the impact the Art-to-Art program created and to give an idea how it made a difference, he congests it all from a big picture record:

"Art-to-Art started with one school each in Ohio, Indiana and Wisconsin. It began to soar and in 2006 peaked itself at a 42-state, over 400 school participation. Using numbers based on the print medias where the program's participating schools were located and its annual national show sites, an unaudited twenty-year history about the program falls within a potential exposure of 50 million."

During AAPJ's initial years, it was published at various print cycles: quarterly, bi-annual, annual as well as in-between special editions. In the latter part of 2003, the *Art-to-Art Palette Journal* began incorporating news and features outside its service to the Art-to-Art program from across the United States and beyond its borders.

In 2010, AAPJ began a full-scale conversion process to present its print format of all its Sections and Departments online - arttoartpalettejournal.com as well as introduced its sister publication, the *Art-to-Art Marketplace Guide* which reports current happenings.

"There are distinctive differences between the Palette and the Guide in regards to what flag the readings will be published under," said Rayman. To point out the specifics, they are noted in the Media Kit:

Art-to-Art Marketplace Guide promotes the services, products and venues for those in and serving the Arts and Educational communities. The Guide is published in print, except included in digital editions.

art to art

Marketplace Guide

Vol. I No. I   A co-membership publication for those in association with the Arts and Educational communities $1.35

ANNOUNCEMENTS

ALL WORD LOVERS WELCOME - ACPW is made up of area poets and writers, and anyone else who shares a love of writing. Meetings are held on the second (or middle) and last Fridays of each month at 6:30 pm at the **Arts Depot in Abingdon, Virginia.** Those in attendance can share their work for a friendly but constructive critique from others in the group. In reading their works, emotions can range from the hilarious to the tearful. For this group of creative spirits, the rule is: there is no rule. Attendance at the monthly meeting varies from a handful to over twenty and the experience level ranges from those just beginning to write to published authors who are often able to lend valuable insights and suggestions. All people who treasure the magic, beauty, emotion, and power of words are invited to attend the meetings. No fee for these meetings. Group has also conducted readings at the Washington County Public Library, Zazzy Z's and other venues. For more information, contact **David Winship** at 276-623-5643.

The **Wassenberg Art Center** presents classes and workshops for adults and children throughout the year. For information on these and other art center activities, visit the website at www.vanwert.com/wassenberg and click on "Calendar". Class offerings are posted as they are set up by the art center's instructors.

Lincoln Highway art sale at the **Century Center.** June 19 - 20, 2009. www.lincolnhighwayassoc.org.

Riverside Art Center in Wapakoneta, Ohio offers an array of classes and workshops in various areas: Art & Coffee, Decorative Art, Colored Pencil Drawing, Beginner & Intermediate Watercolor, Children's drawing, Yoga, Drawing from Life, Exploring Collage, Adult Ceramics, Creative Kids Camp, Oriental Brush painting, Throwing on the wheel, Oils, Pencil Drawing. Also, "Studio Nights" is every other Monday of the month, from 6:00-9:00 pm for members to gather socially, relax and complete existing projects at their leisure. Call Pam Knoch at 419-738-4916 for upcoming calendar dates.

INNOVATIONS CLASSES in the visual arts and wellness for children and adults. Dance, painting, ceramics, and more! Call or visit Arts Place to register. Students may sign up for a session, semester, or ser. Scholarship funding is provided by Dr. G's Memorial Scholarship Fund, MainSource Bank, and Medical Consultants P.C. Call or visit **Arts Place,** 131 East Walnut Street, Portland, Indiana 260-726-4809. M-F 10:00 am - 9:00 p.m. Saturday: 2:00-5:00 p.m. or more info at www.artsland.org

The Blue Ridge Arts Council, Inc. is a 501 (C) 3 designated non-profit arts and education organization that primarily serves residents of Front Royal/Warren County in Virginia. Our programs provide Arts Education, Art Exhibits and Community Partnerships like our Gazebo Gatherings Summer Music Series, which offers a variety of art experiences and entertainment. For membership fees and other information, call 540-635-5988 or www.blueridgearts.org

1100 Chicago Avenue - Goshen, Indiana - Open Mon-Sat. 10:00 am-5:00 pm - 574-533-8900

Sycamore Fine Arts

The AAMG Sections are: Cover Section;
Paletteboards Section and its Departments: At the
Centers, At the Museums, At the Galleries and At
the Libraries; Two Sisters Bookmart and its
Departments: Book Reviews and Reviews-Other; Art
-in-Performance Section and its Department:
CountryStyle; and the Professional Court Section.

Art-to-Art Palette Journal print Sections and
Departments are: Cover Section; Main Section; Paint
Box Section and its Departments: How-Do-It and
Tips & Techniques; Potter's Shed Section and its
Departments: How-Do-It, Tips & Techniques and
People, Places and Events; Bugle Section and its
Department: Educator's Row; Storybook Section and
its Department: Poet's Corner; Cupboard Section;
Clothesline Section; In-Out Design Section;
Centerstage Section; and Back Porch Section.

Today, the *Art-to-Art Palette Journal* continues its
platform, as well as in conjunction with its other family
imprints, serving as a visual 'historical' validation
document about those who have made a difference in and
for the Arts and Educational communities. ♥

"A Quiet Night"

www.ingramcontent.com/pod-product-compliance
Lightning Source LLC
Chambersburg PA
CBHW071358300726
48976CB00006B/1924